MW01236228

Copyright©Marcel Emerson 2018

ISBN 978-1-5323-7390-9
I. The Library
Printed in the United States of America
Publisher: Datruth Publications
Editor: Kevin Dolloson
www.marcelemerson.com
marcel_emerson@hotmail.com
Cover design: Rich Rocket
Layout: Datruth Publications

Dedication:

To: My Family, Friends and Readers

I am excited to be back with another novel. I've always enjoyed horror stories and thought it was the right time to write one of my very own. Thank you so much for your support as I continue to write stories that push the envelope, and shed light on a group of people that have been in the shadows for far too long.

Heidi—

Thank you so much
for your continued
support. Enjoy!

The Library

a novel

By: Marcel Emerson

"If you starve a dog for too long, it will bite you."

~ *Unknown*

PROLOGUE

The library was quiet, which was normal for a Friday afternoon. There, however, was activity in the lower level men's restroom that would change the trajectory of four very different individuals' lives forever. Pablo, Chaka, Curtis and Arnold all had very different reasons for being at the library today. The quartet was standing there in awe, with their eyes transfixed on the mirror that was hanging from the wall of the restroom. Each one of them trying to make sense out of what they'd just witnessed. They couldn't understand how it was possible for someone to reside inside a mirror. None of them actually believed that ghosts or spirits roamed the earth. However, they knew that they weren't crazy and what they'd just witnessed was real.

Angel the young man who had been trapped inside the mirror for over sixteen years, desperately wanted out. He was only a teenager when the entrapment occurred. Angel's soul was being held captive in a world between hell and earth. He would stop at nothing to obtain the magic that would release him from his prison inside the mirror. He'd been lured into the library under false pretenses, not knowing that it would end in his captivity. Angel's years of confinement had stripped away any innocence and virtue that he'd had left. In order for him to be released, Angel had to perform a multitude of living sacrifices to the lord of darkness, and in doing so would give his captor the needed power to break the curse.

Angel's body was gone forever, but once he'd satisfied his debt to his captor he would be given the opportunity to choose a host and possess their body as his own. Angel had just been given the news that he'd almost satisfied his debt and on Halloween the transformation would occur. Angel had a huge decision to make, because the person whose body he chose to possess, he would then live out the remainder of his life as that person. Angel wanted to ensure that the person he chose would benefit him in more ways than one. They had to be attractive, in good health and shape. Angel didn't want to become just anybody, he was looking for a suitable host. Someone that would give him an edge up in life.

The four individuals in the restroom were all suitable hosts all except for one, the only female, Chaka. Angel most definitely wanted to come back as a man, but he could only choose one. He hadn't yet decided between Pablo, Curtis or Arnold, because each of them possessed qualities that he liked equally, but they were all so very different.

Chaka, the only female, appeared to have powers that could potentially derail his plan. Angel was caught off guard and was hoping that it didn't ruin his chance of life on earth again. Angel feared that Chaka's powers could be strong enough to vanquish him before he had an opportunity to take over a body. Angel was hoping that Halloween would hurry and get here before Chaka was able to get rid of him and for good.

CHAPTER 1
PABLO

I woke up this morning on the floor of my mother's small shack in Los Minas, in the capital of the Dominican Republic, Santo Domingo to be exact. They say Los Minas is the most dangerous part of the capital, and we don't get too many tourists venturing into our part of the city. At twenty-two I thought that I would have left this small island and moved either to Spain or somewhere in America. I am the only one of my mother's children who completed high school and attended the University. I couldn't believe that I was back on this hard floor, after winning a spot on my country's Olympic team in track and field.

I'd been waiting for that moment ever since Coach Diego took the time to introduce me to the hurdles my freshman year of high school. He saw me running during one of my gym classes and was certain that I had untapped potential. However, track and field wasn't the only thing that coach Diego would later think I would be good at. Along with track, Coach Diego introduced me to a whole new world of fast money, and foreign men. At that time, I was ignorant at the fact that there was a thriving market of men who traveled to my island to meet young boys like myself. Coming from a large family, in which I didn't receive a lot of one-on-one attention, I was just excited that someone had taken an interest in me and said that I was good at something.

It wasn't necessarily my first choice to do the things that I had been doing with all these men the past six years of my life. However, Coach Diego said that it was a means to an end. He would always tell me if I worked hard in school, and on the track, that I wouldn't have to do it forever, like some of the unlucky men on my island. Coach Diego convinced me to participate in the sex trade, by informing me that I would be able to take care of myself and my family in the process. Living in a household with four other brothers and sisters, with both parents in the house, and all of us sharing one bathroom wasn't something that I wanted to do the rest of my life. Especially after meeting some of the wealthy men who traveled to my island, and hearing their stories of lavish and luxury lifestyles. I too wanted this for myself.

I longed for a better life for myself, and I also wanted to take care of my family. Being the middle child, I wasn't coddled as a child and I was pretty much left alone to do pretty much anything that I wanted to do. Therefore, when I started spending so much time away from home, and with Coach Diego, I didn't get any questions or concerns from either one of my parents. I could only assume my parents were just excited that I had finally found something that interested me, and got me out of their hair.

Everything seemed to be going according to plan with my life. I began to look at all the men Coach Diego would set me up with as friends. I had several repeat customers who would come to the island two maybe three times a year. Not all of them were bad looking either, but they all wanted my attention. This was a very powerful feeling that all these men chose me, to fulfil a fantasy that I assumed only I could fulfill. I was naive when I first started out. It seemed like the younger I was the more men wanted to spend time with me. This was a major ego booster, and I started to think very highly of myself and my looks. Not really understanding that there was something deeply wrong with a grown man wanting to have sex with a teenager.

My first sexual encounter was with Coach Diego. This happened when I was around sixteen years old. He was all I could think about after the first time. Coach Diego was tall, and he was very fair skin. I later found out that his grandmother was a Jewish refugee that came to the island in the nineteen-thirties, after escaping Nazi Germany, and later married his Dominican grandfather. I remember growing up and hearing how being lighter was better, and I would see how the Haitians in my school were treated so poorly. Many Haitians that l grew up around were darker hued, compared to the native Dominicans. My own father would tell my sisters that they'd better not come walking in with no Haitian boyfriend or they would be disowned.

There was this young Hattian boy who was friends with my older brother and used to come to our home. My parents treated him fine, because it wasn't that they didn't like Haitians, they just didn't want their grandchildren to have to be discriminated against and have a harder life than necessary. However, this Haitian kid spent a lot of his time trying to assimilate into the Dominican culture. I think he just wanted to be like everyone else around him. Unfortunately, he was found hanging from a tree; having been lynched for impregnating a young Dominican girl from my neighborhood. The girl was later found dead, and my father would make sure my sisters wouldn't have this same fate. My father would constantly remind them of this once they got to puberty.

I had to admit that I was raised to prefer lighter skin over dark, which was what attracted me to Coach Diego. Not to mention, he had the perfect physique, and he was an authoritative figure who took a special interest in me during a time when I was vulnerable. I remember, like it was yesterday, the day Coach Diego took my innocence away. He had changed me forever, and I was a willing participant.

It was after practice and all the other students on the track team had left, and went home. I remember it like it was yesterday. I was on my way home and Coach Diego stopped me and said, "Pablo I need for you to stay late and work on your jumping technique."

I smiled and said, "O.K. coach." This was something that I welcomed. Any extra alone time with Coach Diego was right up my alley. After everyone left, Coach Diego started showing me some exercises.

Coach Diego was looking at me a little different today. I wasn't sure why, but I just listened. "Pablo," he said. "These exercises will build up your stamina and also allow you to jump higher." During these new exercises I remembered him touching me more than he had ever done before. This was getting me excited, and I didn't know how to control my desires.

The touching was way more delicate than he had done in the past. After we finished working out Coach Diego said, "Pablo let me give you a full body massage. That way you won't have a lot of aches and pains when you wake up in the morning, from working muscles you've never worked."

Not thinking anything of it, I said, "Ok, sure no problem." Then I jumped on the massage table that was located in the back corner of the men's locker room.

When Coach Diego walked to the table he said, "No Pablo, I need for you to get completely undressed and to lay on your stomach." I was shocked and embarrassed by his request because I was already semi-erect from all the touching he was doing during the training. However, I followed his request and quickly stripped down to nothing and rested on the massage table. Coach Diego started massaging my ankles and working his way up my legs. In my head I was like, *"Does he know what he is doing to me?"* When his smooth hands had gotten close to my groin area he didn't stop massaging, nor try to work around my private area. At this point I was completely erect. I was breathing real hard and I could hear Coach Diego seductively saying ever so lightly, "Just relax Pablo, what's going to happen next has to be between us. You trust me, don't you?"

My head was positioned in the head rest of the massage chair, with my eyes shut. I suddenly opened my eyes and looked up at Coach Diego. He too was completely naked. He was standing over me with an erect, red-tinted penis poking in my direction. I was shocked because his penis was lacking the foreskin that my brothers and I had. Coach Diego later told me that he was circumcised at thirteen, which was part of his grandmother's Jewish faith. Over my heavy breathing I muttered out, "Yes Coach I trust you."

Coach Diego then said, "Good now just turn over on your back, and continue to lay flat and enjoy this experience. I've been wanting to do this for months." When I turned on my back I was fully erect. My member was a lot longer and thicker than Coach Diego. I was surprised and thought it strange, since he was older and taller than I was. I would later find out by Coach Diego that he considered me blessed in that region of my body. He told me I would soon see the privileges this would provide me in the near future.

A few seconds later, Coach Diego began stroking my member, and spitting on it—making it moist. The friction was sending me to a state of ecstasy. I was so green; at the time I assumed his hands had gotten tired because he put his mouth around my member and started going up and down. Feeling this sensation for the first time, sent electricity through my body. His mouth felt a lot better than his hands, which I thought couldn't get any better. At this point my breathing was uncontrollable. I was dumbfounded by the experience. I wasn't understanding what was going on, but was frightened and excited at the same time. Just when I thought things couldn't feel any better, Coach Diego puts a condom on me, hops on the massage table and starts riding me like I was a stallion. I couldn't believe how much pleasure I was receiving from a full body massage. All I could think about at the time was that I hoped he, and I could do this after practice every day.

While on top of me, Coach Diego was stroking his own member. A few minutes later his load released all over my chest, and little bit of it splattered on the tip of my chin. This wetness and the friction of his insides on my manhood made me explode in the condom. In tandem, I released a loud roar like a lion. I was sixteen so I had experienced an ejaculation before but only during masturbation. I had to admit, though, it was nothing compared to what I had just experienced with Coach Diego, and I didn't want it to end.

After we both released our loads, I was sitting on the message table in love with my track coach. I laid their speechless, and watched Coach Diego get up from on top of me, cleaning himself off and getting dressed. There was an awkward silence before Coach Diego started letting me know the reason for what had just happened. He smiled and said, "I've been watching you ever since you were a freshman. There was something about you that I immediately knew you would fit right into the track team, and what I have planned for your future."

I looked at coach and was like, "my future?" I grew up Catholic so homosexuality was wrong, and forbidden in my household. I knew my parents wanted me to marry and have kids and continue the Hernandez legacy. What future could the two of us really have? Even though the thought of living happily ever after with coach would be a dream come true, but the likelihood of it wasn't anything that I could really imagine at that time.

Coach Diego continued, "You are very special and from what I just witnessed, you will be very successful at your next phase in life. You see I have a lot of connections in the track world. If you do what I tell you, you could someday go to the Olympics. You will also be able to do a lot for your family financially. You already have the physical capacity; and with my training and connections, you are well on your way."

I wasn't all the way sure what he meant or if I was even interested in his offer. My mother always told me that, "Everything you wanted in life had a price." I, however, wasn't so sure if I wanted to pay that price. This was a lesson that I would learn far too quickly after trusting my future to Coach Diego.

CHAPTER 2
CHAKA

I was always the little chocolate drop in the picture, but as long as I was the cute chocolate drop, it didn't matter too much. However, being dark skin and overweight felt more like a prison sentence, and I was desperately seeking parole. I felt like slimmer women thought they were better than me. When they walked passed me in the mall or the grocery store, the satisfactory looks they would give themselves unnerved me.

I was sitting here now, trying to get my hair done by this skinny African woman, who probably thought I wanted her husband. I guessed she thought all big women were desperate enough to try and sleep with any man who gave them any attention. I didn't have anything against my sistas who were born in the motherland, at all. I remember I was watching this reality show on WEtv about the Atlanta beauty industry for African American women; and I was fascinated with one of the main characters. She was a dark skin sista, just like me. She was born in Africa, had a strong accent, and a strong sense of self. She seemed very powerful and confident in her own right. She was dark, but thin—unlike myself. She owned her own beauty salon and believed in natural hair for black women. I found myself admiring this woman and wishing I could be her.

I made an appointment and flew down to Atlanta to get her to do my hair. I allowed her to put in some natural hair pieces from her new hair line she'd just developed. I loved keeping my hair natural as well, even though I liked to wear extensions. I never processed my hair. When I had left the salon in Atlanta, I had bought about six bundles of the hair because I just loved the texture and the natural feel of it. Also, I didn't plan on flying back down to Atlanta every time I wanted to get my hair done. I had already known an African woman back in Maryland, where I lived, who had done some braids for me in the past. So, I thought next time I wanted to get my hair done instead of flying to Atlanta, my old stylist could hook me up with the hair I had brought back from Atlanta.

It was Saturday and I was headed to a work conference in Houston on Monday. I had made my hair appointment for today, since I was catching my flight on Monday. I wanted a fresh do—who knows who I would meet at the conference. My local stylist, who had done my hair before, didn't really seem all that excited to see me today. I was assuming she didn't appreciate that I hadn't scheduled an appointment with her in a while. When I arrived, I brought in the hair that I had gotten from the salon in Atlanta. I noticed how she was admiring the hair. I didn't think anything of it at the time.

Before she started on my hair she said, "Chaka this hair is wonderful, how much you pay for this?"

I said, "It was around sixteen dollars a bundle," and she started on my hair. Since she was a beauty professional, and this was a new product line, I could see why she was impressed. Shit I was impressed too, which was why I bought this hair, instead of the normal hair I used from the local beauty supply store. Anyway, her husband was also my tailor, and I had still been using his services since the last time she'd done my hair.

I should have known something was wrong when I noticed that she was being really forceful with my hair. I couldn't see what was happening, but I felt like she wasn't applying the hair correctly. So of course, me being me, I made a comment and this bitch had the nerve to snap at me.

She was very condescending when she snapped, "Chaka, do I tell you how to run that library you work at? This is my profession, I know what I am doing." Since she was in my head, I decided to let it go. In hindsight, I should have gotten up from that chair, snatched my hair, and left her damn house.

When she was about finished with the style I wanted, she said, "Oh no Chaka, I don't have enough hair to complete the style that you wanted."

I thought this was odd and replied, "Six bundles should have been more than enough."

She just rolled her eyes and left the room for a moment and brought out some other hair, and said, "Chaka, I can use this on the areas that need more hair."

I looked at that cheap ass hair and said, "No thank you. I don't want to use two completely different types of hair. Please just take some from other areas to fill in the missing areas." I could hear her mumbling underneath her breath, but I just let it go until she was finished with my hair.

When I arrived home my head was itching so bad, and the extensions were shedding. I washed the hair two times to try to get the itching to stop, to no avail. So, I took the hair out because I couldn't go to Houston with my scalp itching as bad as it was. I was so pissed. I had just paid her over two hundred dollars for this bitch to style my hair. I couldn't believe that she had stolen my hair, and decided to replace it with some cheap shit that irritated my scalp.

I didn't know if she was mad that I hadn't patronized her business in a while, or if she thought I was interested in her husband because I used his services more often than hers. I didn't know what was going on in her thick skull, but slim women seemed to always think that they could take advantage of me. I thought about making another appointment with her, and do a no-call-no-show, just to teach her lesson. Fortunately for her I took the high road. I decided that I would take a class that the salon was offering in Atlanta, so I could do the braiding technique myself, and not have to depend on these fickle stylists in Maryland.

There had got to be a way for me to lose some of this damn weight. I had tried every diet imaginable. When Jennifer Hudson lost her weight from Weight Watchers after she won her academy award, I just knew she had found the secret that I had been missing from my life. However, Weight Watchers didn't do shit for me. I was still so big. They say the average size of an American woman was a fourteen. If I could only just get down to that size, I would be okay. A size twenty-two was just way too big, and it was really making me depressed. I didn't even want to date anyone at this point in my life because I felt so unattractive naked.

The only men who seemed to be interested in me were younger men who need someone to take care of them. They were looking for a momma, and Lord knows, I didn't want to be any grown ass man's momma. These youngins didn't mind the extra weight in the bedroom. Especially, after I wined and dined their asses, or cooked them a meal reminiscent of big momma. I wanted a real man though! Not one of these low-life men who thought the world revolved around them. The ones who were content with me bringing home the bacon and cooking it too.

Friends would always tell me, "Chaka be patient; wait on the Lord." How long did I have to wait on my prince charming to arrive? Some of my girlfriends would tell me that I should try and lose weight to get a man. My other girlfriends, who were just as big as me would say, "If he don't want you when you big, then he isn't for you."

I'd heard so many times that, "If he doesn't like you for you, then he isn't going to like you if you lose weight either." I had a hard time believing that, because honestly I have had several skinny girlfriends, and I saw firsthand that they had way more options than I ever did when it came to dating. Men wanted a trophy, especially men with money and prestige. They wanted arm candy, a woman to turn heads, and make their friends envious. Come on, who were they kidding? We all knew men preferred something to look at, over someone kind and practical like myself. Unfortunately being this big, had really taken a toll on my dating life and self-esteem. Shit I was forty-five and hadn't been in a serious relationship in the last thirteen years.

Yeah, I own my own townhome. I'd also bought a single family rental property back in my old neighborhood of Pittsburgh, Pennsylvania. I bought the house right next to where I grew up, and I was so proud, I was able to do this. I also made well over six-figures, and had my master's degree. Some would say I had my shit all the way together, and I wouldn't disagree one bit. I was very responsible, and dependable. I was that sista with stocks, bonds, and a very nice savings account. It made no sense, in my head, that I didn't have a fine ass man and some kids running around this damn three-story townhouse. I was not that picky when it came to looks, but it appeared like all these black men out here couldn't handle a sista like me.

Many of my girlfriends have at least been married, divorced, and had kids of their own. I was like the outlier when it came to them, and I was mad as hell about it. No kids, no man, no prospects, and an empty home and bed at night. Something had to give because Lords knows, this wasn't the life I wanted for myself. Especially at this age when my eggs were drying up, and it was getting less and less probable that I would be able to carry any children of my own.

I had made a conscious effort this year to really start hitting the gym hard and taking care of my body. All the junk I'd consumed over the years was a thing of the past. I was going to cut all the bad stuff out of my diet, and start eating healthier. I would also eat at better times during the day to get my metabolism running like a healthy person, and not a slob. I hated when I overheard folks when they came into the library where I worked saying, "She is so pretty for a big girl." The other sad part was that women would always compliment me on my hair, or my clothes but I very seldom would get any compliments from men. I just wanted a fine ass man to walk up to me, and tell me something about me that they liked other than my personality.

I worked at the Malcolm X Library, in the heart of Downtown, Washington D.C., in walking distance to Chinatown. The Malcolm X Library had the most traffic of any library in the country due to its location and the programming that we scheduled on a weekly basis. I had been working here for the past twenty-five years. I loved my job. When I first started, I was so excited to be working in a metropolitan city, like D.C. I just knew that I would meet a few eligible bachelors either on the job or roaming the downtown streets. In the vicinity where I worked, there was a D.C. office for every blue-chip law firm in the country, the headquarters for some of the largest associations domestic and international, and many governmental agencies.

However, after twenty-five years of hoping and searching, I had yet to meet a guy who could match my intellect, drive, or pay status.

I knew that these guys existed because a lot of my female coworkers were constantly telling me how they had met so and so on the train, or at the nearby Starbucks or Corner Bakery during their lunch hour. For the first five years of working at the library, I had walked around this area with my eyes open, like I was on the Hunt for Red October. I wanted some of the attention for myself. I just knew it would happen. I deserved it, but to no avail.

The few guys who would approach me, were not the guys I wanted. Did I have a sign on my forehead that read, "Desperately Seeking Susan?" It was always the homeless men trying to flirt, all the while asking me for spare change. The unemployed men coming into the library to use the free computers to update his resume would always try and get way too personal. Not to mention, the older, retired men on a fixed income and tired of being cooped up in the house or retirement home who visited the library, always found the time to tell me how beautiful I was. Nobody that I was interested in, which was really beginning to make me second guess my self-worth.

I tried internet dating, from Black People Meet, to E-harmony, to Christian Mingle, and the list goes on and on. Most the men on the internet were undersexed and just wanted some good pussy or some oral sex. These men weren't really looking for a long-term relationship or companionship. Then you had all the married men who had profiles on these sites. They would pretend that they were single, and when you got interested in them and wanted more out of the relationship, they would then drop the "I'm married" bomb as if it now mattered—but of course it didn't when we'd first met.

I also tried dating out of my race too. I had always believed and dreamed of having my very own special dose of Black love. I thought Black love was something that was meant to be for me. However, after meeting so many Black men and coming out of the situation empty handed, I started to think just maybe I needed to broaden my horizons. I had always been attracted to Latin men, with those olive complexions and wavy hair. So, when I had met one who seemed to be interested in me, I said what the hell and gave him a chance. However, he seemed to be needier than the Black men I dated. Not to mention, I couldn't really get with the uncut penis thing. However, I learned to get over that real quick because sex for me had been far and few, in-between. So, as long as the condom stayed on, and he wasn't asking me to go down on him I managed to get through it, but that didn't last long either.

I even tried a long distance relationship with a man I had met over the internet who was oversees in Asia working in the information technology field. It was nice getting to know him over the phone. We had great conversations, I even went to Singapore where he was working a few times to visit him. However, he turned out to be full of shit too. For him it was more about sex and him being bored, being so far away from home. As soon as his assignment was over, and he moved back to the States, I would hear from him less and less, until he just stopped calling and answering my calls.

I tried to keep myself busy by working a lot of hours at the library. I was in a book club that met monthly to busy myself. I did some freelance consulting work on the side for a few nonprofit organizations. I even tried to hang out with my girlfriends, and do cocktails and brunch from time to time. I hated to admit it, but I had this guy who was really good at massages come to the house once a week. Fortunately for me, he would please a sista during our sessions, to get me through the times when I had no prospects, which was more frequent than not. He would always bring weed, which I was also embarrassed to admit it, but the weed and his magic hands were way too relaxing. He had me purchasing my very own massage table after our first session.

I knew this wasn't right, but shit I knew a lot of men who paid for sex. So, I was like what the hell! He was able bodied and willing, and I was in need. Although, this was a temporary fix for my carnal needs. I knew I needed to figure something out, and get back into the dating game and try to find my soulmate. I knew there had to be someone out there who wanted to be with someone like me. I was heavy set and dark skin, but I was always told I was cute for being dark skin. I knew that shouldn't be something that made me happy to hear, but it did.

CHAPTER 3
CURTIS

One of these days I was going to get over the fact that my mother had remarried a man that I cannot stand. I realized that women were totally different than men and that they looked at more than just looks when choosing a mate. *But, damn mom did you have to marry a troll, and a man that doesn't really like your kids that much*? I knew I was a grown man myself. I was twenty now, but I still needed my mom and the support mothers give their children. I wasn't ready to cut the mother-son bond, and move out on my own. However, it looked like I was going to have to, or learn to deal with this new man in her life.

This new man in my mother's life was a doctor. Not a medical doctor or anything like that. Apparently, he had received his PhD in Sociology, and worked for himself as a therapist. My thing with Dr. Wilson was that he was way too controlling, and he thought he knew everything. He didn't know what was best for me and my little sister, he barely knew us. The wedding was less than a week ago and they were currently on a cruise right now in the Caribbean, enjoying their honeymoon. My mother was a school teacher here in Las Vegas, and Dr. Wilson lived in Upper Marlboro, Maryland a suburb of Washington, D.C. Of Course, he wanted my mother to move across the country to be with him. Since my little sister was still in high school she was leaving and moving with my mom as well.

I was currently working in the food services division at the MGM Grand Resort & Casino here in Las Vegas. I had recently dropped out of college because I wasn't doing too well. I started working to take a break, and get my mind right. I wanted to get back into school, but because I wasn't focused my mother thought it was best for me to just take some time off, and not waste money. My mother hadn't known Dr. Wilson for too long. They met only eight months ago, and decided to get married only about a month ago. I thought this was a little too hasty, but I couldn't really tell my mother who had been on her own for quite some time, raising two kids, to not jump at love and happiness.

How and why she could be happy with Dr. Wilson I couldn't understand. He wasn't very attractive. To me, he seemed very bossy, and my mother seemed to be a very different person every time I was around both of them. My mother of course gave me the option to move across the country with her, and my sister if I wanted. However, I could see in Dr. Wilson's eyes that he would much rather me stay here in Las Vegas so that he could continue manipulating and controlling my mother. I hadn't decided what I was going to do yet. Even though I was technically an adult, I didn't think I was ready to be that far away from the person who had given birth to me, and raised me my entire life.

In other news, I had just started dating a guy that also worked at MGM Casino. He worked in the environmental services department though. We would schedule our lunches and breaks together when we worked on the same day to spend time with each other. This was probably another reason why Dr. Wilson probably didn't want me moving with him. He seemed very traditional and old fashioned. Having a gay stepson I was sure didn't really fit in the "perfect therapist's" fat head of his. My mother, on the other hand, accepted me for who I was. She told me when I came out to her when I was sixteen that she loved me no matter what. That was another reason why I didn't want to be that far away because I was truly a momma's boy and before Dr. Wilson I was the only man in her life.

Since I didn't do well on my first attempt at college, I wasn't sure if I wanted to give it another shot, right away. I was up in the air between finding a job once I got to Maryland or school. Dr. Wilson made sure to let it be known that if I was moving with him, I either had to register for college or find employment once I got to Maryland. I was leaning more toward school though. Working at the casino; although it provided me with spending money, it wasn't as fulfilling as I first thought it would be. I did, however, enjoy my coworkers. I knew I wanted to further my education and do something more rewarding with my life. Working with food wasn't my ideal of a dream job, or something that I wanted to do for the rest of my life. Although, I was uncertain what I wanted to do with my life I knew food wasn't it.

There were several colleges in the vicinity where Dr. Wilson lived. I had applied to a few, when my mother first told me she was moving. I had also applied for financial aid, since I didn't have the money to pay for my tuition out of my own pocket. Fortunately, I did get accepted to the University of the District of Columbia. They had a community college arm that sent an acceptance letter almost a week after applying. Unfortunately though, I didn't receive any financial assistance other than loans, because both my mother and father made too much money for any sort of federal grants. Also, since I was out of state coming from Las Vegas, I didn't qualify for any state grants or scholarships.

However, this didn't really deter me because the college did offer me work study. This meant I could choose to work on or off campus depending on the availability. They had sent me a listing of several on and off campus jobs that I could choose from. I thought this would be a good opportunity for me. Go to school, and make a few dollars in the process. I hated being broke. I really didn't know what I was going to do yet. I wished I didn't have to decide so quickly. Why didn't my mom take more time to figure out if this was really what she wanted? She really rushed her decision and this left me in precarious situation.

I know I was being a little selfish, but I was really liking this guy I'd met at work. I didn't want to just pick up and leave after we were having such a good time getting to know each other. I didn't care that he worked in environmental services, which was fancy for janitor or custodian. He didn't look like any of the janitors that I'd ever seen. Boy did he have my nose wide open. His name was London and he too was from Las Vegas, just like me. He was a little older than me, he was twenty-six. He stood about five feet, ten inches, light brown complexion, and had the most piercing brown eyes. When he looked at me, all I wanted to do was melt.

London had a lot of the women on our staff trying to figure him out, and I was shocked when he first showed interest in me. I was certain that he was a player, and had many of the women wrapped around his sexy little fingers.

However, he let me know in the beginning that he only had eyes for me.

When we first met, he looked me in my eyes and said, "Curtis, I can already tell you are a very special guy. I will do whatever it takes to make you mine." Needless to say, he did, and I couldn't help it; I was wrapped up in his spell. London could do no wrong in my eyes, and I was contemplating not moving to Maryland, so I could really explore the possibilities of this relationship.

When I talked to my mother about this, she told me that I was too young to even be considering putting my life on hold for someone that I had just met. If I wasn't such a respectful son, I would have told her, "That's exactly what she was doing with Dr. Wilson," but I held back my true feelings.

During our conversation about London, my mom said, "Curtis baby, what you are experiencing now is puppy love. This is your first love, which is very sweet, but these types of relationships very seldom work out." I didn't know what to think about my mother's advice, because when London and I were together it seemed like I'd known him all my life, and that we would be together forever. Maybe I was blinded by love or just straight up dickmatized. I couldn't put a handle on my feelings, but all I knew was this dude made me weak at the mere mention of his name.

So much was going on around me; it had me confused and a little scared. Lord knows, I didn't want to be so far away from my mom and my little sister. The other part didn't want to walk out on someone who had really awoken a fire inside of my heart and soul that I never knew existed. I kept telling myself what London and I had, had to be the real deal. We talked about any and everything. I could be myself around him. He knew my fears and weaknesses; and never once did I feel embarrassed about sharing anything with him.

If I did stay in Las Vegas, London was offering me a place in his small apartment to reside until we saved up enough money to get a bigger place. I could also stay with my father and my step mother, but they had two younger children—my half brother and sister. I knew I would get stuck being a free baby sitter if I moved in with my dad. Besides, my dad was a retired Veteran. Having been in the military most of his life, he'd become very strict and mundane. He knew about my sexuality, but he couldn't really wrap his fingers around it. He had asked me about it, because my sister was mad at me one day and she told my dad, because she knew I was afraid to talk to him about it.

My dad said, "Curtis, I just don't understand why two grown ass men would want to be with each other sexually instead of wanting to be with a woman. Women are soft and smell good."

I replied to my dad and said, "Dad, you will probably never understand. I don't understand fully myself. I just know what I like."

Then he said, "Sounds like you're confused to me son. Anything you do in life that is important to you, you should always fully understand it and be one hundred percent comfortable with your decision." I just left the room to ponder my dad's words. I loved him, and I wasn't about to get into a debate about something he clearly didn't understand.

I had some really important life decisions that I needed to make and fast. I just hoped that I made the right decision and my life could get back to a more peaceful state. Something told me that life for me wasn't going to be as peaceful as I wanted it to be no matter if I stayed here in Las Vegas, or moved across the country with my mother, sister and Dr. Wilson. I was really torn between the two, but I was certain that whatever I decided, I knew I had to grow up and start being a man.

CHAPTER 4
ARNOLD

I been loving the game of basketball ever since my father put a basketball in my hands. I made my first three pointer at the age of five and there had been no stopping me ever since. Now I couldn't remember ever not playing and loving basketball. Everyone thought I should have dropped out of college and gone straight to the NBA once I became eligible. I'd been wanting to go to the NBA ever since I could remember. So after my sophomore year of playing at Duke, when I became eligible to play professionally, all the top agents wanted me to drop out of college.

It wasn't a surprise to most, because agents and scouts had been trying to lure me into playing professionally overseas ever since I'd graduated from high school.

However, it was really important for me to get my degree, because I was the only one in my family to go to college and my grandmother, who I love dearly, said that she would be so proud of me if I received my degree. My grandmother was so sweet, she was like a second mother to me, and since she was getting older I most definitely wanted to please her as much as could.

The money and offers were hard to resist, but school was something that I also excelled at. I loved to learn and find out about things that I knew nothing about. So, obtaining my degree was something that I looked forward to as well. In just a few days I would be a college graduate, with a degree in English from one of the top schools in the South. Not only was I about to graduate, I had also been drafted in the second round of the NBA draft by the Washington Wizards. My life had been nothing but a dream come true for me.

You could clearly see, I was used to getting everything that I wanted. I also didn't apologize for it. I worked hard, obeyed my parents, and kept my nose clean all these years. While I watched others in my family and neighborhood succumb to drugs, clubbing, partying, and sex. I was busy busting my ass, practicing on the court or reading a text book. I knew the path I wanted for my life. Fortunately for me, I was proud to say: I was well on my way.

At twenty-two, I was already a millionaire. I just signed a seven year, twelve-million-dollar contract with the Wizards. You could only imagine that this had me and my family on cloud nine. You see, I came from a working-class family from the South. A small town in Arkansas named Dermott to be exact, in Chicot County. The only high school, which was Dermott High, had won the state championships all four years I was there. I cherished my roots and humble beginnings, because you have to remember where you came from. My high school continued to represent for the state trophy every year since I been gone. I was proud to admit that I'd started a legacy that had gone on way past my years.

Things were not easy for my parents or my parents' parents. However, they made out the best they could. Growing up, I'd helped out my family by picking cotton at the cotton gin that employed many of the men and women in my town. Picking cotton wasn't a fun thing to do growing up, but it was a means to an end for my family and other families in my town. That was why it was so important for me to get my education and get drafted into the NBA so I could help my entire family, and maybe later my entire community.

As soon as I received my signing bonus, I bought my parents a $150,000 home in the suburbs of Little Rock. I told them they wouldn't ever have to work again. I wanted to buy them a much bigger home, but my father forbade it. He wasn't all that comfortable with taking handouts from his son. My dad was a proud southern man. You see, you can get a lot of house in Arkansas for what I paid for my parents' home. Moreover, since I paid all cash, I was able to purchase a quick sell property, well below its value. It was a four thousand square-foot, new construction, single-family home that only had one previous owner. The owner didn't live in the home longer than a year, because they had gotten a job offer in a different state, and needed the money for their new home.

My parents' new home felt brand new to me. The home had all the amenities that you could think of including stainless steel appliances, granite counter tops, and bamboo floors in the common areas. The house was spectacular, and my parents were happy to live there, and I was happy that I could do that for them.

My college teammates were throwing me a party last night in celebration of my draft, and upcoming graduation. There were so many women at this party trying to get me in the bed. I guessed now that it had been announced I made the "pros," the gold diggers were on the hunt. I usually had my fair share of the fine women on campus; white, black or yellow. However, now they were just way more eager to get me in the bed. For whatever reason, though, these women didn't do it for me. I didn't know who I was fooling by entertaining the advances of these women.

I had been with a small select few women while I was in high school and college. I had to honestly admit that women didn't satisfy me like I felt that they should. I hated to admit this to myself or anyone, because that would mean I wasn't normal. But, after every sexual encounter with women, I would still be all hot and bothered. I remembered when one of my teammates and I had shared an attractive blonde freshman year. She was more than eager to be with her first Black man, and she didn't want to have just one, she wanted two. She confessed to the both of us that her parents had banned her from dating black men in high school, and that this only made her want a Black man even more when she'd gotten to college—away from mommy and daddy. I didn't know what it was about college, but I think that was where you had the freakiest sexual experiences. Not to mention probably the most sex in your lifetime.

I wasn't really all that interested in satisfying her curiosity. However, my teammate Carl was overly excited about the offer. At the time, I'd thought Carl had one of the sexiest bodies that I'd ever seen on another man. So, I was more than eager to take part in the threesome just to get an up-close encounter with Carl. During the orgy, I let him have most of the fun with the blonde. I mainly sat back and watched. Most of the time, the blonde was giving me head, as I watched her take Carl's big girth up her fat pink vagina. I managed to brush my legs against Carl's legs a few times, and both our members touched a few times will we were both receiving fellatio. Those were the highlights of the experience for me. For a whole month after, I couldn't get Carl's gigantic member and nice physique out of mind. Later that night I had the wildest dream about Carl and I. We were both pleasing each other, very lustfully and passionately— minus the blonde. When I woke up the next morning from the dream, I laid there in bed with my boxers wet from the fantasy, pissed that it was only a dream.

If only the dream was reality. I wouldn't still be here with these lingering desires about wanting to be with another man. I'd never talked about this to anybody, and it was something that was really eating me up inside. I felt like I couldn't be myself and that I was living a lie. I wasn't naive. I knew, the professional sports world wasn't ready for an openly gay ball player. As much as the world was progressing, there was just no room for gays in male dominated arenas. Look at Derrick Gordon the first openly gay basketball player to play in the NCAA division one league. He made it to the big tournament three times, and won the Big East Championships with his team. He didn't get drafted into the NBA nor was he playing oversees professionally. You could also look at Jason Collins who was the first openly gay NBA player. Once he announced to the world that he was gay, he was ostracized and soon after retired from the game. Collins later opened up about how bad he was treated by his teammates, and owners after his announcement.

I was sure there were more players out there who were gay. I was also sure that after hearing about Gordon and Collin's stories, any other gay players weren't as quick to come out the closet. In my case, I had my family to look out for. A lot of people were depending on me, and I needed this opportunity. There was no way in hell that I would be the poster-child for gay professional athletes. As teammates, we shower together, and get dressed in front of each other. These hyper masculine men that I played around, would feel uncomfortable knowing that another guy could potentially be sizing them up and wanting to sleep with them. I always steered clear from drama, and I wasn't about to take on such a significant burden.

However, I didn't know how long I would be able to fight off these urges. I'd been fighting them ever since I'd reached puberty. It had gotten so bad that lately I'd been watching a lot of porn, especially male on male porn. Some of the stuff I'd witnessed watching these videos were making it even harder to resist my sexual desires. I had even been thinking that, just maybe I could meet one guy. It would be perfect if he had just as much to lose as I did. We could maybe start a friendship with benefits type of deal, and see how that worked out between the two of us. But unfortunately, I didn't know where in the world I could find this imaginary person.

I thought about creating an anonymous profile on some gay apps that I'd seen in the app store of my phone. I never got the courage to create the profile, though. I kept worrying that I would wind up running into someone crazy or someone who would try and blackmail me or blow my cover. For now though, I would do my best to curb my appetite for men and hope that one of these women from another night of celebrating with my teammates would be able to satisfy my urges. It would be nice to at least have a threesome again, but Carl was two years older than me and was off in Europe somewhere playing ball oversees. When he graduated and moved across country two years ago, I thought I was going to die.

How I found myself in love with a man that had no clue I had feelings for him was borderline crazy, and I knew it. I'd always considered myself sane and level headed, but when it came to matters of the heart, I guess my brain allowed for a little coo-coo. I swear, though, I didn't think I was going to make it the months after Carl left. I mean he didn't even keep in touch. I'd emailed him a few times, and hadn't received any sort of a reply. However, I guess now that I made it into the NBA, I was sure he'd be trying to get in contact with me.

Carl always said that I would make it to the NBA. That was why I was shocked that he didn't keep in touch after he left. He believed in my ability and he would joke around about me being his little brother. Even though I looked more of the big brother than he did. I was six-feet, five-inches and two hundred pounds, and Carl was a shy away from being six feet and one hundred and eighty pounds. He had light mocha colored flawless skin, to my midnight dark complexion. Hell, I would take him being my play little brother right now. Shit, anything to have him back in my bedroom, with any one of these fine ho's who will be sure to be sweating me later on tonight.

CHAPTER 5

It was a hot and humid August day in the Nation's Capital. Many folks were headed back to school and to work after their summer vacations had just ended. Chaka being the busy body that she was, was busy trying to get the programing and events scheduled for the library. Because she was such a micromanager and workaholic, she had come to work early this day just to be ahead of the game.

Chaka was such a busy body and not having any real dating prospects, she was a bit of a worker bee. She longed for the days where she would get off and could go cook for a family or even take her family out to a nice restaurant. She hated coming home to her empty home, so she enjoyed the time spent at work. It kept her busy and her mind off being so damn lonely. Chaka felt that at least at work she was a star and was needed.

Chaka was the go to person for any and everything at the library. She practically ran the library and every person who worked there. She liked to feel needed and work certainly gave her that satisfaction. Since personally and socially she wasn't needed for much. After returning back from Houston, she started feeling like selfish and spineless men treated her more like a watering hole. She had met a man in Houston, who was attending the conference. They enjoyed a few nights of dinner and a movie every chance they got to leave the conference. During the conference, they texted each other nonstop. Chaka just knew she had met the one, she felt love at first sight, and this was actually coming from his mouth. She was just too afraid to say it first.

The last night of the conference they shared their last dinner in Houston. After dinner was done, Chaka invited him back to her hotel room. They enjoyed a wonderful night of passion, filled with promises to keep in touch. They vowed to make plans to get together sooner rather than later. Chaka was convinced she had found her soulmate. It's been two weeks since the conference, and she has yet to receive a text, call back or even a returned email.

Chaka still prayed every night, like she did when she was a little girl, for God to send her, her very own prince charming. Someone to call her own, who loved her physical appearance just as much as he loved her personality. She was determined not to give up on love. Chaka was not a quitter, and she knew love would find her.

Chaka knew there was someone out there for everyone, she just needed to be ready and prayed up, was what she told herself. Not letting disappointment settle in, she dove head first in where she felt comfort—work. The library had just hired a new employee that she was responsible for supervising, and he was starting today. She was excited to be getting some much needed help.

The library often times sponsored foreign nationals to become U.S. residents, and employees of the library. The library believed that finding qualified people didn't just mean looking in just the United States. The library sitting in the heart of one of the world's powerful capital cities, had some of the most diverse visitors than any other library in the country or world.

In order to stay up-to-date and innovative they wanted their workforce to be made up of many different cultures and ethnicities. This meant opening up their hiring pool to the world, and not just the United State. Pablo, who had thought his luck had run dry, had gotten another break of a lifetime. After being released from the Dominican Republic Olympic track team and being black balled in his own country because of the scandal, he had thought his life was over. Now that Pablo had this second chance, he was trying his best to forget and move on. Pablo really hoped that this move to the United States would allow him to start over and get his life on track.

When the offer letter arrived at Pablo's parent's modest home, he couldn't believe his eyes. He didn't have very much work experience, having run track all throughout high school and college. He didn't need a job during this time because he supported himself participating in the prostitution ring that Coach Diego had introduced him to. However, Pablo knew that he was a fast study. Fortunately for him, his English was very advanced, having spent countless hours entertaining American and British men alike. He was ready for a clean slate. He wanted nothing more than to refrain from turning tricks, but unfortunately in order to get the money to move, and have a place to stay, he had to call upon a client or two that lived in the states.

Pablo made it to the states, had a job and was ready to change his life for the better. When he entered the library it was eight fifteen in the morning. He didn't start until nine, but he was far too excited about this new opportunity. Pablo didn't get any sleep the night before, and he arrived early to work. When Pablo walked up to the library, he was astonished at how big it was. As he entered the vestibule of the library, he felt a certain energy that rushed through his body. He didn't know what to make of it, but something about it frightened him. Pablo didn't believe in the supernatural, so he chalked it up to nervous energy.

The library didn't open until nine, so Pablo found himself not able to enter past the vestibule. A few minutes later, a security guard noticed Pablo standing outside the main entrance and said through the glass, "We don't open until nine." Looking down at his watch he continued, "You are a little early sir," pointing to the hours that were stenciled on the entrance door. He then asked, "Is this your first time visiting the library?"

Pablo looked up and through the glass entrance while the security guard was talking to him, and replied, "I am a new employee, and I start today. I am supposed to ask for Chaka Howard. She should be expecting me, but yeah I am a little early."

"Oh Miss Howard, she is here already let me call her for you."

"Oh no, I don't want you to call her right now, she may be busy. I was a little excited, so I got here a little early. I'll just wait right here until it's closer to opening time, and then you can call her and let her know that I am here."

"Well, since you work here, come right on in and enjoy the air conditioning. Go on ahead and walk around. Get to know the facility a little better. I know it's a lot to take in right now. This is your first time here, I am only assuming."

Pablo looked at the security guard as he walked into the library and said, "Yeah, you're right this is my first time. I've never been in a library this big in my life. It's as big as some of these office buildings here in Downtown D.C."

Pablo then decided to venture into the vast, open area of the library. The open space as you walked in was brightly lit. You could look up and see the many floors that the library housed. For a while, Pablo stood there in awe taking it all in. He decided that he was going to find the nearest restroom, which led him to the lower level of the library.

He saw signs for the bathroom once he got down to the lower level. He noticed that there were no windows anywhere on this level. He then thought to himself that, *it would make since that this was some sort of basement and built underground. Therefore, there couldn't be any windows underground.* It was very creepy, because any other time Pablo wouldn't be worried about seeing windows. The lower level was like a maze. It was very difficult trying to find the restroom. You found yourself walking down one corridor that looked the exact same as the corridor that you just walked through. Luckily Pablo found the restroom, which was at the end of the fourth long corridor. There were motion sensors in the restroom. As soon as you walked in the restroom it went from pitch black to as bright as a surgical room. The maze and the darkness of the restroom, before the lights came on felt a little eerie to Pablo.

Pablo, for the life of him, couldn't understand why the bathrooms would be located so far away from the entrance into the basement. As scary as this bathroom felt, he wished the exit was a little closer just in case he needed to get away. Pablo knew that he was the only person in the bathroom, since he had turned on the light from the motion sensor, but he didn't feel like he was alone. While he pissed at the urinal, he looked around the bathroom and underneath the stalls to see if he wasn't alone. He took a deep breath, and thought, good there was no physical signs of anyone present in the bathroom, but yet he kept hearing someone's voice.

Pablo thought he was going crazy as he searched every nook and cranny of the men's restroom. The restroom wasn't that big and there was nobody he could physically see. He decided that he needed to get out of there and fast, besides it should be time to start his new job. When he reached the door to the bathroom he couldn't open it. This freaked him out, because the door flew open upon entry. It was one of those doors that moved forward and backwards depending on if you were entering or exiting. So, the fact that it wouldn't move forward for him to exit didn't sit well with Pablo. Pablo started to panic as the voice he kept hearing started to feel like it was getting closer and closer, and he still couldn't see anyone in sight. Suddenly the lights got pitch black in the restroom, and the door swings open with force.

Pablo ran back through the maze and instead of taking the elevators he flew up the stairs, and back to the main lobby of the library. He didn't know what the hell had happened down there, but he was for certain that he wouldn't be going back down there if he had any say.

Most of the morning Pablo had been so busy in training and trying to keep up with his new boss Chaka. Chaka talked a mile a minute and she was OCD. Pablo had forgotten all about the morning debacle in the men's restroom in the basement of the library. Things had gotten back to normal, or so Pablo thought; and now it was time for his first lunch break. He decided to head toward the McDonald's next to the Capital One arena. He'd walked passed it this morning as he was exiting the train and walking toward the library. Pablo didn't have very much money, so he was delighted when he saw the McPick 2 menu items. He couldn't wait until he received his first paycheck from the library. Pablo was a little nervous about having enough money to last him. If he ran out he was unsure how he was going to manage.

Pablo didn't want to have to start turning tricks for a profit again. Not now that he had a legitimate job. He was in the United States now; the land of opportunity. He figured the last thing that a college educated person, with a decent job should have to resort to was prostitution. However, things were kind of expensive in the Nation's Capital. He had been looking online at apartments for rent; and again he didn't know how he would be able to manage. Unfortunately, since the library sponsored his work permit and immigration paperwork, the pay wasn't the best. Had he lived in the Dominican Republic and made his current salary, he would be living like a king; but not here and not now.

Pablo ate his meal and chilled during the remainder of his break. As he was heading back to work, and obviously not paying attention, he accidently bumped into Arnold, who was just leaving the Capital One Arena, in the opposite direction. Arnold had been there all day with the rest of the new players touring the facility, receiving their player badges and key cards. Arnold felt legit, he now had private access to the arena during game days. He was in such a good mood, he didn't think anything could bring him down. As he was walking Arnold spotted someone that made him do a double and triple take, in the McDonalds that was attached to the arena.

Arnold felt like a peeping Tom, as he stopped dead in his tracks. He couldn't believe that Pablo was the spitting image of Carl. He just knew that they had to be related or something. As much as Arnold wanted to forget Carl, since he didn't have the decency to keep in touch. He still had Carl's face and body in his memory bank, even though it had been more than two years since he had laid eyes on him.

After the two men bumped into one another, Pablo looked up and said, "Excuse me! I didn't mean to almost knock you down?"

After hearing Pablo's accent, and realizing it wasn't Carl, Arnold was a little disappointed. He'd really wished he'd bumped into his old teammate, he really missed Carl. However, Arnold kept up a positive front and said, "It's no problem at all. You must be in a rush somewhere so let me get out of your way."

Pablo replied sensing that the guy wasn't ready for him to leave just yet. He knew he couldn't stay and chat though. Pablo needed to make a good impression for Chaka, so he said, "Yeah it's my first day on the job, so I have to be on time. Don't want to get fired on my first day." Then off he went, on his way back to the library. Pablo didn't look back or even wait to see if Arnold had anything else to say. Pablo at first glance wasn't in the least bit attracted to Arnold. Pablo had a thing for light skinned men and Arnold was a little too chocolate for his liking. Pablo did, however, catch the wanting looks coming from Arnold. Pablo knew enough to know when someone was interested in him. He received that sort of attention all the time, from both men and women.

Arnold, though, still intrigued with his new acquaintance, made sure to stay several persons behind Pablo as he followed him to his workplace. Arnold didn't have to be at practice for several more days and he had more than enough time to kill. When Arnold saw Pablo walk into the library he said to himself, *got you my sexy new Latin friend*. Arnold didn't know how he was going to make sure he ran into Pablo again, but he knew he was going to do everything in his power to do so.

Arnold had just leased a penthouse apartment in walking distance from the Capital One arena and the library. It was only August and basketball season didn't officially start until the middle of October. Arnold made up his mind on the spot that before he became a D.C. public figure, and recognizable to the public, he was going to figure out the best way to get familiar with his new Latin lover. Arnold stood outside the library and watched through the glass entryway as Pablo got lost in the vastness of the large library. Arnold was astonished to see a library this big right smack in the middle of downtown Washington, D.C.

After a few minutes of looking through the glass entry way and into the library. Arnold couldn't leave well enough alone. He found himself going through the metal detectors and entering the library. There was something about the library that was drawing him inside and he couldn't understand for the life of him, why he didn't just walk back toward his apartment. Once he entered the library, the same energy that Pablo felt came over Arnold. Arnold had never experienced something overtake him before and he was startled. He didn't know what to make of the energy, but it was very forceful, and he had no control over it.

Arnold wanted to turn back around, but something was pulling him toward the lower level of the library. Then all of sudden Arnold had to pee. Arnold thought it was strange because he remembered just using the restroom right before he left the players' locker room and exited the Capital One arena.

At this time of day, the library was open and in high gear. There was heavy traffic coming in and out the building. There was a lot of activity throughout the entire library. For some reason, Arnold found himself on the lower level of the library. He followed the signs to the restroom, passing corridor after corridor until what it seemed like a lap around a maze. Until finally he located the restroom at the end of the last corridor. He didn't like being down in the lower level. There was a lot of traffic down in each corridor that he passed. Mostly homeless and transient folks loitering the hallways, with nothing better else to do to occupy their day. Arnold felt like everyone he passed was watching him. Many of the individuals had that desperate look of needing help and didn't smell very well. Arnold looked around and he appeared to be the only one on this level that didn't appear homeless and have an unbearable scent to their clothing. They all reeked of trash and from being outside for days without showers.

After passing so many homeless folks on the lower level before actually reaching the restroom, Arnold thought about just heading back to the arena or even his apartment to relieve himself. However, his body had a mind of its own, it was either now or he would have an accident. Arnold couldn't help but wonder why there were so many homeless people in the library at this time. More importantly, why were they all down on the lower level. He thought, *this would be a sure way for someone to get robbed or maybe even injured.* He didn't see any signs of library staff. All the doors leading to the rooms were closed and locked. The only thing that seemed to be open on this level were the restrooms.

Arnold then reassured himself that, *this was probably normal. That the homeless and street walkers needed to relieve themselves as well. What better place than a public library that welcomed everyone.* When Arnold finally used the restroom, he was ready to get out of the library. He sensed that there was something wrong with the energy in that lower level. Arnold tried to get from the lower level as quickly as he could. However, an elderly woman, who looked to be in her sixties and reeked of piss, stopped him, "Sir do you think you can help an old lady out with a few dollars? I am extremely hungry and I have no food or money."

Arnold wasn't going to be stupid enough to pull out his wallet in a sea of homeless people. He looked around and they all had this dazed, haunted look behind their eyes. He replied, "I left my things upstairs including my wallet. I wish

I could help you, but I don't have any money on me at the moment."

The woman looked right through Arnold and smirked. She had this all knowing look on her face. "Now young man, Arnold is it? How are you going to come down here and lie straight in my face? Didn't you just sign a big ole fat contract with the Washington Wizards?"

As soon as he heard the lady utter his name, Arnold ran so fast down the corridor and up the steps, and back to the main lobby of the Library. He didn't know how that woman could have recognized him. Then again, he thought, well maybe she was a sports fanatic and watched the NBA draft. Arnold assured himself that she had to have kept up with sports to know who he was. All he knew was that he had to get out of the library and fast. To him there was something eerie about the place and he wanted no part. Even if Carl's look alike worked there. Arnold knew he wouldn't be returning back to this library ever again, so he thought.

Arnold was rushing so fast out the library that he wasn't being careful and bumped into Curtis who was walking inside, the library, for the first time. Curtis had just left the financial aid office at the University of the District of Columbia. He had received the approval from his financial aid counselor that he was eligible to do his work-study at the Malcolm X Library. Curtis had finally made up his mind and decided to move to Maryland with his mother, and sister. He accepted the offer and enrolled into the University of the District of Columbia. He was exited that he was able to start work so soon, with the library having one of the only jobs open at this time.

Arnold being the gentleman that he was, apologized for not paying attention. Arnold said to Curtis, "Excuse me man, I wasn't paying attention. Sorry for almost knocking you down. This place gives me the creeps and I am trying to get out of here as fast as I can."

Curtis couldn't imagine a library scarring a man that looked to be about seven feet tall, but he didn't want to offend the guy and said, "Oh really? Well I am headed in myself. It's no biggie, though, I caught myself before falling. However, as tall as you are you could have easily trampled all over me. Thank goodness, I was watching where I was going, and I am good."

"Well don't let me stop you," Arnold said. "Enjoy your visit and be careful there is something really weird about the lower level of this place. Enter at your own risk, but don't say I didn't warn you," Arnold remarked and walked away as fast as he could out the entrance of the library. He left Curtis staring at him in lust.

It had been a few weeks since Curtis had left Las Vegas, and he was missing his boo, London, already. Cutis wouldn't have minded if Arnold did a quick stand in for London. Curtis was missing the regular sex he was having with London, before he'd departed Las Vegas, which had put him on a sudden sexual drought. Carl and London decided that they would break up. They both weren't too happy about having to do a long-distance relationship. London had tried to convince Curtis to stay in Las Vegas, but at the end of the day Curtis knew he needed to change his environment. More importantly, Curtis wasn't ready to be that far away from his mother and sister.

Chaka was all smiles after meeting both Pablo and Curtis. They both appeared to her to be good additions to the library. They both seemed bright enough and eager enough to be on her team. She was a no-nonsense type of boss; however, she was fair, so as long as you came to work on time and did what was asked; she didn't see why the three of them wouldn't get along.

Chaka also admired how handsome both Pablo and Curtis were in their own right, respectively. She had been around the block a few times. She had her own gay friends and going by her judgment, she assumed they both were homosexuals. She didn't bring it up because it wouldn't had been professional, but she made a mental note to herself. She also thought, staying quiet about her assumption was the best thing to do, last thing she needed was to get in trouble for sexually harassing her employees. Chaka knew herself very well. She was a very up-front person, and she had the tendency to be in your business if you let her. After meeting both Curtis and Pablo, she started to wonder why most guys she met in this area were all good looking but gay. She hadn't met so many gay men in her life before moving to this area. She was glad for her "gaydar," though, because some of these gay men were fine as hell, she thought. The last thing Chaka wanted to do was get caught up falling in love with a man, who was secretly into dating and having sex with other men.

Chaka introduced Pablo and Curtis to one another, after she showed Curtis to his work station. She also informed Pablo that he would be supervising Curtis and signing his timesheets. Chaka thought they looked a little too happy to be working together, after just meeting. She wanted to also inform Pablo and Curtis the rule against fraternizing with coworkers at the library. However, since it was their first day she left well enough alone. Chaka knew that Human Resources would be covering this, along with a list of other do's and don't's in their orientation soon enough. The main reason she kept quiet was she didn't want to offend either one of them in case her "gaydar" was off. Chaka felt like she had psychic abilities and her judgement was very rarely wrong when it came to men. Gay women on the other hand, unless they were the dominant, or overtly masculine they weren't that easy to clock. But with men, even if they were supposedly on the down low, she could always figure it out after a small conversation.

CHAPTER 6
PABLO

The library turned out to be a fun place to work. There was so much to do and so many different people who came into the library, I barely had a dull moment. My boss, Chaka, was a piece of work. I could tell she knew that I liked men but for some reason, I always felt like she was flirting with me. However, these feelings could just be in my head, and judging from the past two weeks being at the library, it appeared that Chaka flirted with any and everybody.

I had managed to stay away from the lower level of the library after that first frightful day. I didn't tell anybody what had happened or what I had witnessed down there. Especially, out of fear that folk would probably think I was crazy. However, I knew something was down there. It was nothing but pure evil, and once I got enough nerve, I was going to figure it out. Not today though, it was Labor Day weekend in the United States and that meant I had a three day weekend. Coach Diego, for some reason, wasn't ready to let me go and live my life. Even being in the Dominican Republic and me being in the United States he still thought he could represent me; or for lack of a better word, he still thought he was my pimp.

Considering me being kicked off my home island's Olympic team and everything that happened afterwards, I would have thought Coach Diego would had moved on to someone else. Not so fast, I guess he was still the same greedy and selfish person I had met all those years back. Even though he masked it in the beginning with attractive looks and charm. However, considering that living in D.C. was a lot more expensive than I had anticipated, Coach Diego had caught me at a vulnerable point and made his offer way too hard to refuse. Coach Diego had connections to a billionaire from Dubai that would be visiting Las Vegas over the Labor Day weekend. He had seen pictures of me and was excited to meet me in person. The escorting lifestyle was a hard cycle to break. Considering the money was a lot easier than anything that I had ever done before to make a living for myself.

The only thing that you could call hard about sex work, was that I had to get hard enough to receive fellatio and maybe penetrate my many clients. Luckily for me, me being the one being penetrated was very rare. Many of the guys who paid for sex were too drugged up and could barely keep an erection. If the trick wasn't attractive and I couldn't get myself hard the natural way, there was always performance enhancement drugs. The problem with that, though, was it would keep me with an erection for several hours, even after I had released, and my services had been rendered. This new, rich Arab client had already given Coach Diego five thousand dollars to secure my airfare, and a room at the MGM Hotel and Casino, Las Vegas.

I had worked my full shift at the library and had packed my bag the night before my departure. As soon as I had left work, I took the train to Ronald Regan National Airport in Arlington, Virginia, and boarded my flight to Las Vegas. I had never been to Las Vegas; but coincidentally, the new work-study student, Curtis, was from Las Vegas. Curtis was nice enough, but he seemed to be more on the depressed side for my liking. I was not too much older than he was. I couldn't imagine somebody being from the United States with so much opportunity and being that unhappy. I know he left his friends and family to move to the Washington Metropolitan area, but he was young; he would make new friends.

Curtis did, however, give me a few places to frequent while I was in Las Vegas, which I thought was nice enough. I was excited to get to see more of the United States, even if it did have to deal with me escorting. Folks have been paying for sex since the beginning of time, so what I was doing wasn't something new. I tried not to feel ashamed, but it was just degrading. Some of these men had the worst personalities. It made perfect sense that they had to pay for sex. When I first started doing this type of work, I had a hard time looking at myself in the mirror, after I'd let someone touch me just so that I could receive a few dollars. I also didn't like the person this profession was turning me into.

I was turning mean and angry at the world. I always seemed to have a quick temper. Flying off the handle any chance I got. I allowed the smallest things anyone would do or say to me, that I didn't like, get to me. I would most certainly cut you before I would allow you to cut me. I knew this came from having to dumb myself down and allow these men to do and say whatever they wanted to me just because they had the upper hand—the money. Some of these guys could be the biggest assholes you could ever meet. They judged me for taking their money for sex and wanted to treat me like I was a piece of meat or an object. I was never really treated like an equal, but I never thought I was their equal either.

These men carried the purse strings and they didn't have a problem letting me know they had the power either. I didn't understand, in the beginning, how taxing this job could be on the soul. I would go home after an appointment and would be so messed up in the head. I would ask myself, why someone would want to pay for me to be in their presence just to demean my character and make me feel worthless? When I tried explaining this to Coach Diego, his only advice was, "Pablo, you need to accept the good with the bad." He even said, "Pablo, there are a lot of folk that wished they could be in your shoes."

Even though I understood that logic, because I also knew that there was always someone worse off than me. But, I was sure nobody truly wanted to have to sell themselves and have sex with people to put food on their table or to live. My personality had gone through the wringer; my innocence was nonexistent. I had become a very calculated, manipulating, and self-absorbed person. My relationships with my siblings suffered. We allowed sibling rivalry and petty beefs to get in the way of what could be a beautiful family bond. Although my insecurities ran deep, I acted as if my shit didn't stink. I couldn't keep any real friends or a real boyfriend, because all I could think about was how I could benefit from the situation. I was for certain, if you looked up opportunist in the dictionary, in any language, you would see a picture of me.

I thought somehow by moving to the United States, I was given a second chance. However, every chance I'd gotten I'd reverted back to my old crafty ways. You would think after that traumatic experience with the Olympic committee, I would have learned my lesson. I still had a hard time talking about the experience. Even though I had a hard time sleeping at night, because I laid awake replaying the events over and over in my head. The saying "no sleep for the wicked" was my moniker. I didn't believe in God, because the devil wouldn't let loose his grip, and I wouldn't release him. I knew I needed to change my ways, but life was just too hard, and this money was just too fast and too easy to give it up.

Las Vegas turned out to be very routine for me. I was put up in a very nice hotel suite, with access to unlimited room service, and access to all the fine amenities the Hotel had to offer. Lastly, I didn't have to exert too much energy with my Arab billionaire. He was too busy boasting about how he made his fortune in oil, and how many wives he had back in his country. It felt like the sex was an afterthought, which didn't bother me one bit. Not to mention my client stayed high on meth the entire time, and couldn't keep an erection. I was so glad when he said he had to leave. He had to attend some meetings for the conference that brought him to Las Vegas in the first place. Of course, he said he was always in Washington, D.C. and asked if he could see me again after tipping me very handsomely.

Now that I had completed what I had come to Las Vegas for, it was time for me to explore the city. I still had one full day left before I had to board the plane and head back to D.C. to resume my life. Las Vegas reminded me somewhat of a playground for adults with the elaborate buildings, all the best restaurants, casinos, entertainment; and not to mention, legal prostitution. There should be no reason why any adult person shouldn't have a good time in Las Vegas. There was certainly something for everyone and that included me.

I decided to head out to a nightclub to see what the Las Vegas nightlife was all about. Curtis recommended that I checked out a club called the Garage, and when I looked it up it was in walking distance from my hotel. When I got to the club it was already packed, wall-to-wall with gay men from various backgrounds and colors. The music was blasting with the latest dance tunes. This was most definitely the place to be on a Sunday night in Las Vegas.

After several drinks and dancing with this straight white woman from Kentucky, I was thoroughly enjoying my stay in Las Vegas. My new dance partner was in Las Vegas for her and her best friend's bachelorette party. She kept me occupied almost the entire night, saying that I was the cutest guy in the club. Right before the club closed, I was finally able to get away, and see what the men were up to at this place. I decided to grab another drink and stand over near a large speaker where a muscle-bound man wearing nothing but a speedo was gyrating on top of the speaker. The eye candy I was observing was very welcomed, as I scanned the room to see if there was anyone in it that I wanted to bring back to my room. Then suddenly before I could catch anyone's eyes I felt someone grabbing my arm.

Before I turned my head, I was hoping that it wasn't the inebriated white woman from Kentucky looking for me to head back onto the dance floor. But to my pleasant surprise it was a tall brown skinned slender fella, vying for my attention. I smiled and gave him a flash of my pearly whites. Letting him know, without saying it that I was excited that he'd gotten my attention. It was always nice to flirt and be with someone where the attraction wasn't forced, and it was mutual. In the back of my head, I was thinking if I was lucky enough, I would be entertaining this guy one-on-one. I knew for damn sure I wouldn't need any sexual enhancement drugs, because he'd already excited me with just his voice.

My new friend and I decided to head back to my hotel room after a few more rounds of drinks and grinding on the dance floor. The grinding was getting so seductive I could feel his manhood rising on top of mine, as our bodies rhythmically pressed up against one another on the dance floor. Also, when I was twerking on him—something I'd picked up in the clubs since being in D.C.— all I could feel was something hard pressed up against my backside. So, when he asked to come back to my room, I was more than elated to take him up on his offer.

Before I could even get all the way in the room, this new guy was kissing me very ferociously on my neck. I knew the next morning I would have a hickey where his lips and teeth were nibbling. Normally this would have been a deal breaker, but something about how passionate and excited this guy was turned me on. He was so damn aggressive, and his "take control" attitude turned me into putty in his hands. I took a backseat to anything and everything that he wanted to do.

When he pulled off all my clothes and positioned me ass-up-face-down, I was so relieved that I had cleaned my insides thoroughly before heading to the club. When his tongue entered me, I could had sworn he was a lizard. His tongue went so deep, deeper than some of the men I had let penetrate me. His ass eating skills were the best, and he was enjoying me like I was a prime cut steak from the most expensive and delicious restaurant in Las Vegas.

He suddenly stopped pleasuring me orally and gotten undressed. When he did, his manhood stood at attention, and it was the thickest and longest I'd ever seen. It was a good thing that he had tossed my salad for so long. He had me extra wet. After he put the condom on, I couldn't believe how this big piece of meat entered me with ease. I was sure it was the combination of the liquor and excitement that allowed him to enter me so easily. This guy was so long winded; we stayed in the missionary position for at least an hour before he and I both released simultaneously. I wasn't ready for him to go, after he'd released. I wanted more, but he said unfortunately he had to be at work in less than two hours. I pleaded for him to stay and call out.

As he was preparing to leave, I pleaded one more time. "Don't go sexy. I don't even know your name, but I've never experienced what we just encountered together. You're like some sex god, I want to have sex all morning until I leave, what will it take for you to stay for a few more hours?"

He replied, "You have worn me out, with your insatiable sexual appetite. But, I am so sorry I wish I could. I shouldn't even be here now. I actually work for this hotel and if anyone sees me leaving your room I could be fired. Give me your phone. I will put my name and number in it, and hopefully we can see each other next time you are in Las Vegas. You're the sexy one by the way. What are you Puerto Rican or something? I hear an accent."

I replied, "No, I am Dominican."

"Same thing," he said. I let that go, normally I would have cursed someone out for calling me Puerto Rican.

I watched his sexy ass throw his clothes on haphazardly, and walk out of my hotel room, after kissing me so gently on the forehead. When he walked out the door I grabbed my phone, so I could see what his name was since he never once uttered it to me the entire night. My new friend's name was London Webb, and his number was 702-555-1213. I went to sleep with a huge smile on my face. Glad that I'd visited Las Vegas and hoped that something brought me back very soon.

CHAPTER 7
CHAKA

If it wasn't one, thing it was another. I swear I thought that by becoming a landlord it would be a great investment for me. Not to mention, I was able to buy the house next door to the house where I had grown up in, in Pittsburgh. I never imagined it would be such a headache; especially because I hired a property management firm to manage the property because I lived about a five hour drive away in Maryland. God forbid I complain to anyone in my family about this headache—everyone was such a hater. Mad that I was successful enough to own two homes. We all were raised in the same family, so if I achieved this success, anyone could have as well. My parents never picked favorites; we'd all had the same tools growing up.

I didn't mind renting to family at first. That later turned out biting me in the ass and looking like the bad guy after it was all said and done. I allowed my sister to live in my place and she just stopped paying rent. So, like any good business woman would do, I had to put her ass out. I was sure if I breathed a word to my family that these new tenants that I now had weren't paying rent, all hell would break loose. All I would hear was "I told you so," or "you should have worked with your family more." However, I knew it was a mistake to do business with family in the first place. Especially when they thought that because I didn't have any kids, had my master's degree, and a good job that I didn't need their rent money. As if I made an investment so that my sister and her kids could live rent free, hell no. They had me fucked up. That was why they had to go.

I thought by putting a white family in my home things would be a little different, and for the first ten months or so, things kind of ran smoothly. Now, not so much anymore. I had some major concerns with this new family, but it didn't have anything to do with them not paying their rent, in the beginning. You see these motherfuckers thought they owned my home. I specifically had it in the lease agreement that I didn't want any pets. This family had not one, but two big ass dogs. I wasn't a heartless bitch or anything—I didn't ask them to get rid of their dogs when I found out that they had gotten them. However, I did ask for them to provide me with a doggy deposit. I thought this was fair, and far within my legal rights as the owner. I knew all too well how dogs could fuck your shit up, and there was no way I was going to let them off the hook. Of course, they paid the deposit, after I threated to evict them if they didn't either get rid of the dogs or pay the deposit. Ever since the dog incident, though, there had been one issue after the next.

It had gotten so bad that today these tenants got my Black ass driving all the way up there for court. I was fed up with this family at this point, and I want their asses out of my place. If it wasn't one thing it was another, and now I just needed them out. Ever since I sent them a letter to vacate they haven't been paying rent. The property management company decided to part ways with my contract with them too. They said the situation between the tenants and myself had gotten way too complicated for them to manage the property effectively. It was such a horrific situation, I couldn't wait to settle this case.

I couldn't believe the management company just dropped my property from their roster. I mean really, you're supposed to be in the business of managing properties and tenants from all walks of life and backgrounds. You can't handle these crazy people? They better be glad I wasn't in court today suing them for breach of contract. Good riddance to them and their three percent management fee they collected each moth from the rent. What was really boiling my blood and why I decided to take these losers to court wasn't their failure to pay rent. They also had the nerve to change the locks on my doors!

I had my brother go over and check the place out about a month ago or so. The tenants had been complaining that there was a leak in the kitchen coming from the roof. I'd given them ample notice that I was sending someone to look at it, so I could get it replaced or repaired. It didn't matter the price; whatever needed to be done. However, I had a warranty on the place, so anything that needed to be repaired would be taken care of. They just needed to have some patience and give me time to get someone out there and access to the house.

When my brother arrived, nobody was there. He then tried using the keys that I had just overnighted to him, the day before. The keys didn't work to any of the doors to the house. I had him take a picture of the locks because I knew what the old locks looked like. Low and behold, my stainless steel locks were replaced with some fake gold cheap locks. I picked out every door, lock, and fixture in that home. I knew my taste and those gold locks were not it.

They had no right to change anything in my place, and try to keep me out? What they thought I was going to come in and steal their shit? Needless to say, that was the last straw. I was hoping that this judge would do his civic duty and give them notice to vacate like yesterday. When I arrived at the courthouse, my lawyer was already there outside waiting for me. I didn't like the look on his face. He seemed to be annoyed and was rambling on about something on his phone. I walked up to him, just to let him know I was here and ready to get this chapter closed in my life.

Frantically, my lawyer said, "You will not believe this. The wife is seven months pregnant, and their lawyer is a young attractive black man. We have an uphill battle to conquer in this courtroom today. Be prepared for the unexpected, and please remain calm, we don't want to come across as angry."

I walked into the courtroom and looked to the left and I saw my white tenants sitting at the table in front of the courtroom with all four of their kids looking pitiful. The courtroom was not a place for children, but I guess everyone had to have a gimmick. Their lawyer looked to be in his early thirties. He was well dressed with an impeccable smile. He shined those pearly whites at my lawyer and I as we passed the defense table. Although the smile was warm, you could feel the coldness of his soul through his eyes. I wasn't in the mood for pleasantries, so I nodded and took my seat to the right.

A few minutes later, the bailiff was asking the courtroom to stand while the judge made his entrance into the courtroom. I had already known that I was going to have a white man as the judge. My lawyer had prepared me for this as well. It didn't actually set in until I walked in the courtroom and saw that poor white family on my left. It was still a little unsettling, because I grew up in Pittsburgh and unfortunately white privilege still prevailed in this part of the world today. I sat down, did a silent prayer, and let my lawyer do his job.

"Your honor, thank you for hearing our case today. My client, Ms. Chaka Howard would like to regain possession of her home. She has been renting to the Mullens family for thirteen and a half months and they don't seem to be on the same page. The lease, which is a part of the court documents, specifically states that, 'there are to be no pets allowed on the premises' and the Mullens have at least two dogs. My client has had to deal with a lot of disagreements, and unresolved situations. The locks were changed without her consent. To make matters worse your honor, my client has experienced very rude, and unprofessional behavior. All she is requesting is that she be paid the remainder of the rent that is owed. Lastly, she would like for them to vacate the premises, as soon as possible. Hopefully by the end of the current month. The defendant has not paid the last three months of their rent, which they agreed to in the lease agreement. To make matters worse, your honor, they refused to vacate the premises after their lease had expired three weeks ago."

My lawyer went down a laundry list of things that he was hoping would persuade the judge to rule in my favor. I felt like he was doing a stellar job and I was hoping that the judge thought so too. When my lawyer finished his opening statement, the Mullens' lawyer started his case against me. "Your honor the Mullens are a hard-working family. You see they have four children and one on the way. They have gone through a very traumatic experience renting from Miss Howard. They are constantly being harassed by her and her family members. When something needs to be fixed or replaced, it takes her more than it should to rectify the matter and my clients are left suffering. As the court can see from her legal residence, that Miss Howard doesn't live in close proximity to the property. She lives all the way in Maryland, and neglects her landlord responsibilities; as a result of being far away with no adequate assistance.

"Miss Howard agreed to allow pets on the premises. We have a copy of the pet deposit agreement and check that was made out to Ms. Howard. She talked about the locks being changed. This is far from the truth, my clients have never and would never change any locks on the doors. The Mullens do plan on vacating the premises, however, due to Mrs. Mullen being about to give birth to her fifth child, the timing is really bad. The family needs more time to do so. We are also counter suing Ms. Howard due to the timeliness of the repairs. The constant harassment that they have been experiencing has had a lot of stress on Mrs. Mullen, she is scared that she may miscarry at term. Nobody, should have to go through what this family has been going through from their landlord. I've attached a police report dated two months ago to this date, which my clients had to file. They were being threatened to be put out on the streets and the locks to be changed if they didn't move out. Your honor this type of behavior should not be tolerated in your jurisdiction by any respectable landlord. These out of towners want to buy houses in Pennsylvania, because it's cheaper, but don't want to put in the work necessary to be good landlords. Why should the people of this fine state have to deal with the likes of Miss Howard?"

I almost couldn't control myself. What was this lawyer talking about? *I wasn't an out of towner. I grew up in the house next door, asshole.* I wished I could have screamed that out in this courtroom, but I knew it wouldn't help my case one bit. I couldn't believe the lies that they were making up about me. The Mullens were sitting over there looking like they were this upstanding family. And, they weren't the ones who had tormented me these last few months. I didn't know how my lawyer planned to retract all the bullshit, their lawyer had just spewed out. He'd better figure out a way since I was paying him two-hundred and fifty dollars an hour to handle this case.

The judge asked me a few questions as well as the Mullens before we recessed. The judge dismissed us for lunch and said we would reconvene in an hour. I could barely breathe by this time. I was so mad that I couldn't keep from crying. I couldn't believe these bastards were trying to sue me. To be honest with myself, the shit the Mullens were coming with did sound believable. Me being a single Black woman, with no kids, and two properties I knew the judge wasn't going to feel bad for me. He was looking at all those mouths they had to feed. Not to mention the fact that they were white, wouldn't work too well in my favor.

Needless to say, when we reconvened the judge granted the family ninety days to stay on the premises. He also excused their back rent and ruled against me on the countersuit saying that all parties should be satisfied financially with his ruling, which made absolutely no sense to me since I let them stay rent free. I guess the judge thought he was being fair by saying that the Mullens had to pay the current rental rate for the three months they had to find a new place. I was mortified. I didn't know how in the world something like this could happen in America. Not to mention all the money I lost renting to these people. My lawyer told me that I could appeal the judge's decision. At this point I just needed to get out of this court room before I went postal and killed somebody.

CHAPTER 8
CURTIS

I was really home sick and missing London like crazy. I didn't realize how much I would miss him. I called him every day and we texted non-stop throughout the day since I'd been in Maryland. However, it didn't make up for not seeing him. I wanted the real thing. I missed his hands on my body. His lips against my skin, and the way he would make my body shake during our love making. I knew my mom thought I was too young to be this much in love. Love didn't really have an age attached to it. When you found love, I always thought it was best to keep it real close and hold on to it. Wasn't that the same reason why my mom moved all this way—for love? She was kind of being a hypocrite, but I wasn't going to tell her that to her face.

I couldn't wait to get home to call London to see how he was doing. Although the phone calls didn't really satisfy my sexual cravings. I had to admit that it did feel nice to know that I had someone thinking about me. I had just left work, which I had been enjoying ever since I started. My two bosses Chaka and Pablo turned out to be really cool. Chaka reminded me of my mother—very professional and always busy. I could imagine my mother being the same way Chaka was at work. My mother was a principal at a high school in the new county we lived in, Prince George's County. Pablo was just nice to look at. He was very nonchalant about most things, and kind of elusive. I could tell that he'd been through a lot, because he was a little rough around the edges. Pablo had a temper, and you knew not to mess with him. However, as long as I did my job, those two left me alone for the most part.

Right before I left work I had to use the bathroom. I had to drop some informational pamphlets off in one of the conference rooms in the lower level of the library. There was a meeting that was scheduled for early in the morning, and I would be in class, so I did it before I left. This was the first time I had gone to the restroom on the lower level. It was sort of like a maze down there, but I eventually found the conference room and the restroom. I had to walk from one corridor to the next, but finally there the bathroom was, at the end of the maze. Before I had found the restroom, I almost peed my pants; it was so far down the hallway. There was a weird feeling I got once I entered the restroom. Not to mention it was filled with homeless people taking bird baths. I made a mental note to not use this bathroom again. All those homeless people freaked me out; they all had a dazed look on their face. It was almost as if they were looking straight through me.

The train from the library to the Branch Avenue metro stop, where I was meeting my mom, was a nice little ride.

The ride allowed me to do some much-needed meditation and relax a little bit after a long day of classes and work. My mother was the new principal at the Suitland public high school just a few blocks away from the metro-stop. There were days that I had to sit at the metro stop and wait longer than I anticipated for my mother to arrive. Sometimes she would have me waiting for an hour before she picked me up. This didn't bother me too much because I liked to people watch. Let me tell you, there was a lot of eye candy getting on and off at the Branch Avenue metro stop.

Soon as I got to the stop today, I called my mom. When she answered her phone I said, "Mom where you at? I just got to Branch Avenue."

She replied, "Hold tight baby, I am just wrapping up a few things at the school and I'll be right there." I sat at the benches at the kiss and park area of the station to await her arrival. While I was standing there, I noticed an older gentleman looking in my direction. He looked to be in his early to late thirties. He walked past me a few times. I first noticed him while I was exiting the metro. I didn't think anything of it when he bumped into me slightly and said excuse me as we both ascended from the escalators to get out of the metro.

However, now that it had been more than thirty minutes since I'd arrived at my stop, I was wondering what he was still doing hanging around here. More importantly, why did he keep walking past me? I was hoping my mother hurried up and got here in case he was trying to rob me. Although, he would be in for a rude awakening since I barely had metro fare in my pocket to get to this stop. However, I still didn't want him to even try me. I decided to walk up the block as if I was going to walk to my mom's job.

Then as I was walking away I heard a voice saying, "Do you need a ride? Are you okay? I see you been here for a while, is your ride late picking you up?" When I turned back around to see who was talking, it was the same man that had been making me nervous.

I responded, "Oh, no I am fine thank you. I have a ride that is on the way. She's just running a little behind schedule."

The stranger wouldn't let it go, "Are you sure? I have seen you a few times at this stop waiting for a while. You sure you just don't want to call whoever is coming to get you, and let them know you don't need them to come."

Okay, this was getting to be a little scary. I'd already said no thank you. But, to find out that he'd been watching me prior to today, freaked me out even more. I tried to be as polite as possible, and not offend him. He could be a crazy person for all I knew.

Because I didn't know who he was or how long he'd been watching me on the low I responded, "You are far too kind. In fact, I am waiting on my mother. She would be upset if I left before she got here. I do appreciate your kindness, my name is Curtis by the way, nice to meet you? I am originally from Las Vegas people aren't that nice there. I guess since we are in the South folk look after you here." I was hoping he would take the hint and get lost, but no he kept talking.

"Oh, you're from Las Vegas? I love Vegas. I knew something was different about you, and that you weren't from here when I first laid eyes on you. My name is Jeffrey, and it it's very nice to meet you too. The DMV area isn't really considered the South. People aren't that nice or friendly around here. You do need to watch your back in this area. I just saw you and it looked like you needed some help is all."

Luckily, I saw my mom pulling into the kiss-in-ride area of the station. I was so relieved. I could finally get away from this stalker. "Oh, look here she is right there! Well it was really nice to meet you Jeffrey." I shook his hand and walked to get in the passenger side of my mother's vehicle.

My mother saw the look on my face, and she could tell something was wrong, so she asked, "Who was that man you were talking to out there? He looked old enough to be your dad. What I tell you about these creepy older men? Be careful Curtis, this is a new area and you don't know much about how these people operate on the East Coast."

My mom was tripping! Jeffery didn't look that old, and she knew it. My mom was way too over protective. Shit I was about to be twenty-one in a few months; she needed to relax. "He is nobody mom. Just someone that I ride the train with on days I have to work at the library."

She looked at me and sucked her teeth and said, "MMMMMMH." My mother worked with children all her life. She had this innate ability to sense when children were in danger. She had always been too overprotective. What she failed to understand, though, was her son had become an adult. I was a man and not a child, I think I could handle myself. I tried changing the subject.

I said, "So how was work mom?"

She answered, "Work is so busy these days. I am just trying to get acclimated to the way they do things around here. Sorry, I was late again to pick you up.

"You're fine mom. Trust me I understand." I wasn't about to complain about her being late to pick me up. Since I was grown, I probably shouldn't be relying on my mom to pick me up and take me home every day. I guess this was the reason why she still treated me like a child. I was hoping that I could get a car soon. I was now working, and I decided to take out a few loans for school. I planned on getting a car as soon as I received my financial aid refund.

When we arrived at the house, I did some studying and completed a paper I had to turn in the next day for my English class. By the time I finished the paper, it was getting late. I had an early morning and I should probably get some sleep, but London had been on my mind all day. I felt like I owed him a call since he hadn't called me the entire day.

He picked up after a few rings and said, "Hey baby, I was just thinking about you. If you wouldn't have just called me now, I would have been dialing your number."

It was nice to hear someone was thinking about me too, and I said, "Awe baby, I miss you so much. I been thinking about you all day. I have plunged myself into school and work because I am so lonely without you."

"I miss you so much too baby! Life hasn't been the same since you left. How are things going with you anyway? Are you finally happy you moved?"

"Well, I do like school and working. I feel like I have a purpose now, and I know what I want to do with my life. You know when I enrolled in college in Las Vegas, I didn't do too well because I was too busy partying and what not. I was completely unfocused. Now, I am supper focused. The only thing is, I am so freaking lonely. I miss you something crazy London."

"Awe Curtis, I miss you too baby. I need to pay a visit to the District of Colombia. I know some people there."

"You know some people? We never talked about you knowing anybody in D.C., Maryland, or Virginia. You knew I was moving out here for months, and I've talked with you several times since I been here, and this is the first time I am hearing you mention you 'know people' in this area."

"Baby calm down! I am just running my mouth. You know I don't know nobody on the East Coast, my entire family lives in Las Vegas. When I said I know people I was meaning you, boy. You are too funny." I let that comment go. Maybe he was just joking about knowing people, London was a big jokester. We talked for a while longer about meeting up soon and I fell asleep as soon as we said our, I love yous and goodbyes.

I woke up in the middle of the night after having the realest dream that I could ever imagine. There was this young Black boy who looked to be around high school age. I remember his face vaguely and he was very handsome. I remember him telling me his name was Angel. What was confusing me was he was telling me his life story, but in the dream, he appeared to be giving me the run down in the men's bathroom on the lower level of the library.

Angel started off by saying, "Curtis, I was wondering if your mother told you how special you are because if she didn't she should have. You see everyone needs love. Especially your mother's love. Yeah, I didn't have all that. I wasn't as lucky as you are. My mom was a crackhead, and all she cared about was where her next high was coming from. However, I never let that shit get to me, till this day. I will say, though, I don't know how to love anyone or never had the opportunity. Like you have with London. I don't know how to love, and I am afraid it's too late for me, because all the bullshit I had to endure. My mother was too busy getting high to raise and look after her youngest son."

As Angel was talking, I couldn't help but wonder why it would be too late for someone who looked younger than me to find love? I kept quiet and let him continue talking.

"You see the world doesn't allow you to wallow in self-pity. Nobody enjoys a pity party. Some would describe me as being strong. Strong is like the word power, it means something to a lot of people. Love means something too, and for some reason everything in this life reverts to that word love. You see loving yourself more than anyone can love you, can take you a lot farther than a mother's love. Did I love my mother? Of course I did, but what is love when you don't know what love is?

"You start sneaking away at a young age trying to find something that you don't even know if it truly exists. I found myself searching, knocking on the wrong doors, and becoming a follower. All the while, trying to fulfill a void that nobody has ever given me. You see depictions of love on the television screen, at school; shit everywhere, you see two people together with their eyes locked on just each other. That had to be what love was, so I thought. Unfortunately, it's only been me and I want love so bad it's crippling.

"When I reached puberty, I found myself staying up all night on phone sex lines, gay dating websites, and allowing random dudes to dump their loads in any hole in my body they wanted to. Hoping desperately that I could get them to fuck me enough to love me and receive sexual pleasure at the same time. Because having sex with a man at such a young age—thirteen to be exact—and enjoying it, has turned me into a sex addict. I find myself addicted to the pain as well. All the while getting high, damaging my body, and not giving a fuck. I am scared, and I am wondering is my time about to run out and how long can I lead this destructive lifestyle."

Then "BOOM" I wake up in a cold sweat and the dream is over. Who the hell was Angel, he had to be real? This dream was just too real to be just a dream.

CHAPTER 9
ARNOLD

My adjustment to the professional world of basketball was way more exciting and surreal than I anticipated. I was literally in shell shock when I met the players on my team. I tried not to be that dude, the star-stricken rookie, but I couldn't help it. Most of these guys I'd been following their careers since high school. Being so up and close with some of my idols, was making me a little nervous. I tried my best to compose myself enough to get through practice. I played alright, but it wasn't my best performance on the court. Thank goodness it was just practice.

I was excited because our first pre-season game was tomorrow, and we would be playing the Cleveland Cavaliers. I couldn't believe that my first match up, I would get to meet and play against LeBron James. This would be the highlight of my week I was sure of it. Although, I was on a high with everything I had going on; ever since I left the library, near the arena, I'd been having these crazy dreams. Things were getting a bit scary as of late. Every time I woke up in the middle of the night, I was completely drenched from sweating profusely. I couldn't remember every detail from the dreams, but I do remember a teenage boy. He had taken over my dreams and wanted me to do something. However, I wasn't sure what it was that he wanted me to do. It had gotten so bad I was afraid to go to sleep at night. Every time I closed my eyes the teenager would appear with another story or revelation. I think his name was Angel at least that was what I could remember.

What I could remember from last night, Angel appeared in my dreams and he was trying to get me to go back to the library. He had somehow known that I had followed the young man who worked there and looked like my old teammate, Carl. Now I was regretting following the guy into the library, because I couldn't shake away these dreams. They were getting worse and worse. At first, it was just a story of a young gay boy who had a hard time fitting in. He was from a low socio-economic background. His family barely made ends meet, and he was teased at school because of his worn out and old clothing and shoes. I later found out that Angel was the young boy. I was unsure why he was giving me a glimpse into his life. It was really sad, though. Angel's mother was addicted to crack and he didn't know his father. Every night since I'd left the library I dreamt about this kid. He would not leave my thoughts and my dreams.

I thought about talking to the team psychiatrist about what was going on. But, I decided against it, because then I would have to explain so much about the boy's sexuality. This I knew was sure to arouse questions from the doctor, regarding my own sexuality. I had just joined the team. The last thing I needed was the team shrink to be probing into things I wasn't comfortable with sharing with anyone. I couldn't very well allow this to occur. I was just a rookie and this team had invested a lot of money in me. They expected me to be emotionally, physically, and spiritually sound. I also knew that there was patient-doctor confidentiality. However, I also knew that the owners of this team were paying this health care professional way more than what they would make in the outside market as a therapist. So, my business was up for grabs, especially if it could potentially jeopardize the team and its reputation.

I tried my best to block out the memories while I was awake, but for some reason I just couldn't shake the memories. This Angel was just too real, and he wouldn't let me go. I kept having this unsettling urge to go back to the library too. Not just to see the Carl look alike, but to go to the men's restroom on the lower level. That restroom freaked me the hell out. When I finally finished peeing, I knew I never wanted to return. So, this strong affinity to that place was mind boggling. I was just glad I had other things to focus on like practice, and my first pre-season NBA game as a Washington Wizard's player.

###

The game turned out to be more exciting than I expected. Even though our offense and defense wasn't good enough to defeat the Cavaliers—we lost by nine points —I was still in the best mood ever. Being on the same court as LeBron James was more than enough reason not to feel bad about losing my first game as an official NBA player.

I thought the nightmare that I had the previous night was going to ruin my day. The dream was too real, I knew it had to be true. In the dream, I had watched Angel lure two innocent young men into the lower level men's restroom of the library. I watched how the two men had the most passionate sex that I had ever witnessed between two guys.

It made the pornography that I had been watching as of late, look like soft porn.

The sexual encounter almost had me waking up with a wet dream, but after the two unsuspecting men climaxed, Angel ripped both of their hearts out with his bare hands and ate them like an apple. Then I saw the body and all the blood disappear like nothing had ever happened. By this time my alarm was sounding, and it was time for me to shower and head to practice before the game. I kept trying to get the images out of my head, but it kept replaying like a movie.

I wasn't sure what all this had to do with me and why I kept dreaming about Angel. Was he a real person? Was he alive or was he dead? All these questions remained unanswered as I started my day. I didn't really have much to celebrate after the loss, nor anyone to celebrate with. My parents couldn't make it to D.C. for my first game. My father had to work. My dad still worked a full-time job. He was too proud of man to live off his son.

I remember the conversation I had with my pops, the day the money started rolling in. I said dad, "You know you no longer have to hold on to that job. I have more than enough money to last you. Go ahead and apply for early retirement."

My dad looked at me like I was crazy and said, "Boy, your money is your money. Besides I don't have it in me to sit home all day, doing nothing, no matter how much money I have." I always respected everything my dad said so I didn't protest. Even if I had, he wouldn't have listened anyway.

Of course my mother wouldn't dare leave Arkansas without my father. She was one of them old fashion wives. She believed that the woman had to take a backseat to her husband's lifestyle. So, there was no family support at my first game. I wasn't mad either, since it was really an exhibition game. Both of them were sure to be at my first game of the regular season. Dad had already requested the time off.

There were only three other rookies added to the team this year, and of course their families and girlfriends were there to hang out with them after the game. I had been keeping to myself lately because of these crazy dreams. Also my sexual cravings were taking a toll on me too. It seemed like everywhere I turned, I was undressing men that I found attractive in my head. I would find myself thinking about the freakiest and nastiest things to do with these men. Not to mention all the players on my team that I found myself attracted to. I would go home, turn on my computer and watch male on male porn. I would fantasize about me being one of the men on the computer screen. Something had to give and soon.

I was walking out of the locker room, after the game, when I heard a familiar voice calling my name. I turned around and there was my old teammate Carl walking toward me with a wide smile on his face. He still looked as good as I remembered him. However, he was limping and walking with a cane. It took him longer than normal to catch up to me.

I reached out and embraced him when he got within arm's length and said, "Hey buddy, long time no see. What the hell did you do to your leg?"

Carl replied, "Man I've had so many injuries in the last few years, and I recently just tore my ACL. I had surgery to reconstruct the ligament, a few months ago. I been in a long-term rehabilitation program. I just started walking again. Life isn't as great for me as it is for you. However, I will be fine soon enough, and hopefully I can get picked back up by a team. I still have a few more years left in me."

I was so happy to see a familiar face. I didn't know what to do with myself. I was also equally excited to see my dear friend Carl. I was sure he didn't know how many times

I'd laid up thinking about him. "So Carl, what are your plans for the rest of the evening? I would love to catch up and maybe go somewhere for drinks?"

"No plans at all my friend. I would love to hang out with you. It will be like old times. I know I am not walking as fly as I used to, but I am sure I am still good company," He laughed.

We headed to The Park on Fourteenth Street. I heard this was a place that a lot of the players would go and celebrate after winning a game. Although, my team didn't win I still felt like I had a lot to celebrate. Especially now that I had experienced a blast from the past. When we arrived at the Park we were immediately escorted to a VIP section of the club. Carl made sure of this, informing the door man that I was a rookie on the Wizards roster, and just had played my first game.

Once in VIP all eyes were on Carl and me. We were the new faces and folks wanted to know who we were. Women were trying their hardest to get in our section. Of course, Carl being the ladies' man that he was, didn't mind sharing our quaint little section with the women who he found appealing. He didn't let his injury deter him one bit. He was enjoying the star treatment, more than I was actually. It kind of felt like old times again. Finally, after a few bottles of Patron, I finally got a chance to have a conversation with my old friend.

I asked, "So what really brings you to Washington, D.C., and where are you staying?"

"You must have forgot that I was from Richmond, Virginia, which is just a few miles up the road. After being released from my team overseas due to injuries, and my contract being expired, I'd been crashing on the couch over at my mother's crib. Arnold, staying with my mom after so many years has really taken a toll on my self-esteem. She is constantly nagging about this or that. You would think that after taking care of her since I left college, she would be more open to the idea of me crashing with her until I got back on my feet."

After hearing Carl complain about his situation, the only thing I could say was, "I am so sorry to hear that bro. However, you still didn't tell me what brings you to D.C."

Carl looked at me with those sexy ass puppy dog eyes and said, "Well you know I keep an eye out on what our teammates have been up to. When I heard that you got picked up by the Wizards, I thought maybe I could hit you up for some help. You were always like my little brother to me back in college. I was hoping maybe you wouldn't mind giving me a place to stay until I recover fully from my surgery.

"You know we don't make as much money as you guys do playing oversees. To be honest with you, after helping my mom's out, and just trying to stay afloat, my finances aren't really what they should be. You and I always had such a great friendship, we even hit a few ladies together. I thought maybe you would be the one I could count on since you've been so blessed."

In my mind I knew there had to be something up with Carl, and how he just popped up out of nowhere to come to my game. I mean the nerve of this guy. After he got his deal overseas he didn't even send a text, email, or DM to check on me; or see how I was doing. Now his ass was down in the slumps, and he wanted my help. I couldn't believe this nigga; however, I still had feelings for Carl. He also still looked good as shit, even with a cane and a limp. So, against my better judgement, I said what the hell and brought him home with me after we left the Park. I was hoping and praying that I made the right decision, in trying to help an old friend out.

CHAPTER 10

The library was very quiet since it was a Friday afternoon, which was very normal. Most everyday people wanted to enjoy their weekend and leave the studying, reading, and research for the former parts of the week. Still, the library staff had to work their weekly scheduled hours. Pablo was keeping himself busy by walking around the library posting signs for an event that was coming up. The up-coming mayoral debate was taking place at the library in a few weeks. It was important that the library let its customers know that there would be limited access to the library on that day, due to larger than expected crowds. This year, the first female candidate for mayor, who actually had a shot in winning the race, had women all around the district fired up. Chaka wanted to be sure that the library was prepared for larger than normal crowds. It was a tradition for the first District of Columbia mayoral debate to be held at the library.

Pablo had almost completed posting all the signs he was given, having meticulously placed them on the bulletin boards and restroom doors throughout the library. He was avoiding the lower level restrooms since he too had been experiencing the same dreams that Curtis and Arnold were experiencing. Pablo didn't know what to make out of what was happening to him. The dreams were insane, he thought. He couldn't explain the constant urge to visit the lower level men's bathroom. He had heard stories from a few of the guys that he'd met since moving to D.C. that, that particular men's restroom was infamous for male-on-male hookups. Pablo wasn't into public seedy places to get off. He was already oversexed as it was because of the sex work that he performed.

Pablo remembered one specific conversation that he had with a guy on the train. Pablo mentioned to the guy that he worked at the library near Chinatown. The guy outright laughed and told Pablo, how it was notorious for hookups. He also said Pablo was probably enjoying working there. The last comment pissed Pablo off. Pablo was offended, but it didn't take much to piss Pablo off.

Pablo then changed his attitude quick. He went from flirtatious to psychotic in less than a second. He raised his voice, not in the least bit worried about the other passengers on the train, and went off. Letting the guy know that he wasn't into that kind of stuff, and how he shouldn't assume anything about him since they'd just met.

Needless to say, the guy got off at the next stop to avoid another tongue lashing from Pablo. When the guy left Pablo watched him walk off the train, and thought to himself, maybe I over reacted. This definitely wasn't the first time Pablo had flown off the handle and wasn't going to be the last. However, he did enjoy his job, but that bathroom scared the shit out of him. It wasn't just the restroom; the entire lower level scared the shit out of Pablo. He wanted to inform the guy about his dreams before he got off the train, but he didn't want him or anyone to think he was crazy, so he kept it to himself.

Pablo was pacing back and forth on the main level, afraid to walk downstairs. He'd already placed all the signs around the library except for the lower level. In walked Chaka coming inside the building, obviously from her lunch break. She was sporting a huge grin on her face. She saw Pablo pacing and walked up to him to see what was wrong.

Chaka startled Pablo and broke him out of his trance, "Pablo why are you walking back and forth with those posters still in your hands? I know I gave you just enough for all the bulletin boards and the restroom doors. So, since you still have some in your hands you couldn't possibly be done. But, you should be since you left to do this way before I went to lunch. This isn't like you is everything okay?"

Pablo knew that Chaka was not the one to play with, and as of now he had stayed on her good side. He replied, "My apologies, nothing is wrong at all. I just have a lot on my mind; I will be finished with this task very soon. I just have the lower level to complete and I am done."

Chaka started walking away and said, "Oh, ok well come and see me when you're done. I want to discuss something with you about the event anyway."

"No problem I will be there shortly," Pablo said heading in the direction of the lower level. Pablo hadn't gone to the lower level since his first day. With Chaka on his ass, he decided as he entered the stairwell that he was going to face his fears. He was going to see if this Angel person really existed or was this just a figment of his imagination. When Pablo got to the lower level he saw quite a few people down there in the hallways and to his excitement they weren't all homeless people roaming the hallways.

He was then reminded that every first Friday around this time, the DC Chamber of Commerce had their monthly meeting in one of the conference rooms down here. This put Pablo a little more at ease since something was going on, on this level. He thought to himself, hopefully if Angel is real, he would know better than to show up while all these people were congregated down here. Pablo posted all the signs he had, except for the one that went on the men's bathroom door.

He had one more sign left, and he thought about getting rid of it and avoiding the bathroom altogether, but he didn't want Chaka to find out and he wind up in some sort of trouble. One thing that Pablo had over his head, was that he had to remain at this job for at least three years in order to remain in the United States. He also knew that the likelihood of getting another company or agency to sponsor him was like one in ten million. Pablo definitely didn't want to go back to the Dominican Republic and back to his parent's modest home.

Pablo planned to just put the sign on the door and not enter the restroom, but as soon as he got close to the door it opened on its own. This freaked Pablo out immediately. When he peered inside he saw a tall dark skin man that he recognized but couldn't put a finger on where he'd met this person before. He noticed that the man was staring in the mirror looking to be in some kind of trance.

Pablo entered the restroom to see if the guy was alright. Once he was all the way in, Pablo heard the door slam behind him. Pablo tried to remain calm and said, "Sir are you okay? Why are you just standing there looking like you just saw a ghost?"

Then the lights abruptly turned off and it was pitch black in the restroom. Pablo started screaming, "Get me out of here! What the hell is going on? These are motion sensor lights they should still be on, and there are two people in here."

Then suddenly a light came from the mirror, and directly through the mirror you could see Angel smiling at both Pablo and the other guy in the bathroom. Angel started speaking through the glass and Pablo got quiet. "Yeah I am real, Pablo. I am as real as you and Arnold are. I wasn't expecting you down here today, but I felt your presence when you entered the lower level. You see Pablo, you are the reason why Arnold his here. He was lusting after you, and he followed you to the library on your first day of working here. I have to thank you kindly for bringing someone of Arnold's caliber to my dwelling place."

Pablo had a quick flashback from the McDonalds and remembered that Arnold had ran into him. Arnold was fine enough he thought to himself, I wonder why he just didn't speak. However, he couldn't think about that now he wanted to know what the hell was going on and why Angel was behind the mirror? If he was just as real as they were, why was he behind a mirror?

Arnold snapped out of his trance and said, "What is it that you want from us? Why are you haunting my dreams, and why am I in this god-awful bathroom?"

Angel replied, "I was just about to answer all of your questions, but now I can answer them for the both of you and kill two birds with one stone," he laughed. Angel continued, "You know I love killing, but not birds—men. Especially men who creep around with other men in seedy places like this bathroom. These disgusting men are thinking that nobody is watching and that their carnal desires can be fulfilled by strangers with no repercussions, or commitments."

Arnold yelled out, "We haven't done anything with each other in this restroom. So why are you going to kill us? Is this what we're here for?"

Angel got angry and when he got upset his eyes turned red and his innocent face 'morphed' into something Arnold and Pablo had never seen before, but frightened them nonetheless. Angel transformed into his demonic form, and looking like the devil reincarnated, screamed, "Don't ever interrupt me. I am running this show. But to answer your question: no, I don't want to kill either one of you. Halloween is approaching and every year I get the opportunity to become flesh and blood just like the both of you. In order for me to do that, one of you will have to take my place inside this mirror and I get your life.

"Here is a little history, so you know your life isn't sacrificed in vain. I made a deal with an immortal witch who felt sorry for me the night that I died. She was visiting the library and heard my cries as my attacker tried to kill me in cold blood. She saved me right here in this bathroom. In order for me to reclaim my rightful place on this earth I have to offer up bodies for the blood magic that she performs, which is why I kill. The blood sacrifices have to be substantial enough to open up our two worlds. This will then allow me to pass through, so that one of you can take my place. This can only happen on Halloween night, when the demonic forces of the world are at its peak. When evil is greater than good. There is only one day in an entire year this happens and that is on Halloween.

"I have finally reached enough blood sacrifices for this to become reality and I don't want to wait any longer. I haven't decided which one of your bodies I want to inhabit. You both have some very awesome qualities that I find very endearing. It will be hard to choose between the two of you. Nevertheless, I am sure one of you will make it very easy for me when that time comes."

This revelation sent chills down both Arnold and Pablo's spine. Neither one of them wanted to spend eternity behind a mirror. Trapped forever in a world between life and death. Angel was abruptly interrupted by Chaka knocking on the restroom door. She held the door ajar and the lights finally came on. Chaka yelled, "Pablo are you in here? I been looking all over for you? I told you that I needed to discuss something with you that was important."

Angel had disappeared, and it was just Arnold and Pablo in the restroom. Finally, Pablo responded and said, "Yes, Chaka I will be right out. My stomach started hurting and I think I am getting a bout of diarrhea." That was the only thing Pablo could think of to explain why he was in this restroom for so long.

Chaka not wanting to interrupt Pablo in his sickness, apologized and said, "Okay, I guess what I have to discuss with you can wait until you feel better. I will be in my office until I leave for the day. If you aren't feeling any better go ahead and leave early and we will catch up next week."

"Thank you, and I am so sorry about this Chaka. Whatever you need from me you know I will take care of it first thing Monday morning." Chaka left the bathroom, but she was a little confused because she could had sworn when she opened the door she heard someone else besides Pablo talking. She also heard them say something about blood sacrifices and inhabiting bodies. Chaka didn't want to make too much out of what she had heard and wanted to give her star employee the benefit of the doubt. However, she couldn't help but wonder what the hell was going on in there.

Chaka was excited that the weekend was approaching. Even though her investment property was still giving her a headache, there was light at the end of the tunnel. This had more to do with Chaka's blossoming love life, and nothing to do with her tenants from hell. She had met a man on Match.com, and he turned out to be what the doctor ordered in her time of need. Especially, to get her mind off her current troubles.

Chaka, however, couldn't leave well enough alone, even though she had been in one of the best moods in a long time. She knew she heard someone else in the restroom with Pablo. She had gone back up to her office, but after a few minutes of racking her brain, she decided to go back to the lower level men's restroom. She wanted to see what was going on for herself. When she got to the door of the restroom, she looked underneath the door and didn't see a light on so Chaka knew nobody was in there so she just opened the door and walked right in.

Angel was still inside the mirror waiting for an unsuspecting male couple to come in and do their seedy deed, so he could perform another sacrifice. He was shocked to see Chaka walk in and actually see him staring back at her. Angel knew that women generally couldn't see him other than witches.

Chaka, as for her spiritual beliefs, she was far from a practicing witch. Chaka felt like the practice of witchcraft was from the devil. Chaka, however, was something very special and very rare, but she didn't know it yet. Her father, before he had passed away, was a pastor in the Apostolic Black Church. He was a high-ranking Bishop and was often times referred to as one of the greatest prophets of his time. He was often praised for talking directly to God and spirits that still roamed the earth.

Chaka was born with that same gift, and prior to this day had never came in contact with the supernatural, as far as she could remember. Chaka, however, decided to leave the church a long time ago. She didn't think that religion was her calling, and she was more than a little disenchanted with the Black church. She felt like there was too much hypocrisy and little regard to God and His word.

Chaka spoke first when they both made eye contact, "Yeah, I see you and what are you doing in my library?"

Angel fired off in hostility, annoyed that he had to be interrupted by the likes of Chaka. He replied, "If you can see me, then you should know what I am doing here."

"Well if you won't tell me trust me I'll find out, and you won't be here for very long..." Chaka knew exactly what Angel was. She had been around her father too much not to know. "I am not scared of you demon!"

"Well if you know what is best for you, you better get out of this restroom and never comeback."

Chaka trying to remain in control, like she'd become accustomed to said, "You don't know who you are playing with, and If I were you, I would take my own advice. Leave this restroom and this library immediately and never return." Chaka left the bathroom terrified. She didn't see Angel like the gay men who encountered him did. What Chaka saw, was his demonic form, and this almost made her piss her pants. She knew from her upbringing that a demon could never harm her, unless she had given her life over to the flesh. Although, Chaka didn't attend church as much as she'd wished she did at this very moment, she was fully aware that she was still a child of God and covered by the blood of Jesus.

When Chaka got back to her office she had a flashback to when she was a child and she remembered her father getting rid of something similar. Chaka didn't have all the answers at the moment, but she was determined to get this demon from up out of the library.

While Chaka was sitting in her office, she was still a little bit on edge. She was startled by a light tap on her door. In walked Curtis, he was on cloud nine because he'd saved up enough money from working at the library, and he had bought London a plane ticket to come visit him in D.C. Curtis had just received a call from London informing him that he had just arrived at Ronald Reagan International Airport, and was getting ready to take the train to the library and meet him.

Curtis was there to ask if it was okay to leave a little early since it was Friday and very slow. Chaka being out of it, with her mind on Angel, agreed and said goodbye and said she would see him next week. Curtis was very excited to see London; not only did he mentally and emotionally miss London—his body was missing London's touch as well.

Before Curtis left for the day, he remembered he needed to go to the lower level and make sure the audio visual equipment had been turned off properly and all the expensive equipment was locked up after the DC Chamber of Commerce meeting that was held earlier that day in one of the conference rooms. He was avoiding the lower level and the bathroom altogether since having nightmares about Angel. However, the thought of spending the weekend with London, had him feeling fearless. He was ready to get it over with, and whatever was waiting for him in the bathroom, if at all, he was ready to face his fears.

After Curtis locked up everything in the conference room, he made his way down the long corridor to the bathroom. He hesitated when he got to the men's restroom door. He took a deep breath and walked in. As soon as he walked in, the motion light turned on and he was in the restroom alone. He walked over to the urinals and used the bathroom, so he didn't have to go when he left work. He then went to the faucets to wash his hands. He said to himself, I guess all this scary stuff must be my mind playing tricks on me. There isn't anyone in here trying to kill me or at the very least trying to harm me.

Curtis quickly washed up and was heading out the bathroom when all of a sudden, the lights in the restroom went off and it was pitch black. What the hell, he thought, maybe the maintenance staff needed to change the light bulbs. He then tried pushing open the door, but to Curtis' surprise the door wouldn't budge. He then got frightened and started beating and kicking on the door hoping someone would hear him and try to open the door from the outside. He thought, *where were the homeless-squatters when you needed them?*

He then heard the same voice he heard in his dreams, "Nice of you to finally come and see me. I've been waiting patiently for you to make your way back down to the bathroom. You aren't afraid of me are you Curtis?" Curtis was afraid to turn around to see who was talking. He wanted to dart out the bathroom so fast but couldn't. He tried the door again, to no avail. Angel watching from the mirror continued talking, "Now that you're here, you can't leave until I say so. So, you might as well turn around, face me, and get comfortable."

Curtis did what he was told while shaking frantically, "What is it that you want from me Angel?" Curtis wondered why Angel stayed in the mirror and didn't come out from inside the mirror.

Angel being able to read the minds of all the gay and bisexual men that had entered the restroom said, "There isn't enough carnal energy in here for me to have enough strength to leave the mirror to answer your question. Maybe you should bring someone down here for some sexual pleasure. I am sure I'll be able to come out and play then. You see, I need some action to occur, then and only then do I have the power to escape my prison inside this mirror. I can leave the mirror, but I can't leave the bathroom. At least not yet, in my current state."

Curtis fired off, "What is it you want from me? Why are you stalking my dreams and why are you keeping me locked up in this restroom? I need to go already, damn."

"You honestly don't think I would leave you in suspense now that I have your undivided attention, do you?

You scratch my back and I will scratch your back. I see you're being stalked by a person that I would like for you to bring down here to this very restroom. Jeffrey the older gentleman that you met at the Branch Avenue metro stop, bring him to me, ASAP."

Curtis was dumbfounded, and asked, "How could you possibly know who is stalking me and what his name is? This is getting too freaky for me!"

"I have very special powers, Curtis, and once you enter this restroom I have a lot of control and foresight over those that enter my domain. Unfortunately, you are one of the unlucky ones. However, I will make a pact with you. You bring me Jeffrey and I will leave you alone. I will also give you bit of helpful information about your dear friend London that is waiting in the lobby for you as we speak. Yeah, I know why you are in such a rush. Be safe and don't do anything I wouldn't do," Angel laughed. Then the lights turned on in the restroom, and then Angel was no longer visible through the mirror. Curtis tried opening the bathroom door and to his surprise he found himself outside the restroom.

CHAPTER 11
PABLO

I was so afraid to go to sleep at night for the last few weeks or so. Ever since Angel revealed himself to me and what he planned to do to me if I was the unlucky one, had me wishing I'd never took the job at the library. There was no way in hell I wanted to live for eternity inside a mirror in a bathroom at the library. I'd rather go back to the Dominican Republic and struggle there than to have to deal with that. I wondered if coming to the United States was the right decision. Never did I imagine that there were things like Angel in this world. Shit I didn't even believe in magic, let alone witchcraft, ghosts, or spirits. What was next, was I going to find out that vampires really do exist too?

Although I was scared shitless, it seemed my love life was on the up and up. London had made a surprise visit to the district and we spent a few days together exploring each other's bodies, along with the city. I swear I never had so much sexual chemistry and passion from anyone that I'd ever met. It was a shame that he lived so far away because I really did miss him after the first time I'd met him. It was a shame that he'd left the district too. I was missing him already, again. I will say, though, London seemed a little weird on this visit, and very secretive.

I never really got a clear reason why he was in my area to begin with. Also, there were so many times when I wanted to see him, and he was unavailable. I didn't think anything of it at first, since he did surprise me by coming all this way. I must admit that the time spent was worth it, so I didn't complain. I wasn't trying to rock the boat and start acting like a crazed lover, since we weren't even exclusive. However, the way he fucked me was as if he was my lover, and I enjoyed every minute of it.

Where the confusion arose in my love life was after finally getting to know Arnold, and what we had experienced together with Angel at the library kept us in constant contact. He was the only one I felt comfortable sharing that crazy experience with. Anyone else, I was for sure would think I'd gone crazy and lost my mind. For some reason this situation was bringing Arnold and I rather close and I found myself falling for Arnold too. How could I have feelings for two guys at the same time? I really was being selfish, but there were specific reasons why I liked them both so much.

Arnold and I were both dreadfully trying to make sense of what was going on. Immediately after the incident, I went back to Arnold's place, so we could figure out what the hell had just happened. Come to find out, Arnold was experiencing the same dreams as I was. We had also looked online and found out all the killings we witnessed in our dreams had actually occurred in real life. On the

Metropolitan Police Department's website, each individual killed in our dreams, was listed as a missing person.

The families were looking frantically for their love ones. The website said even if it was just a body, they wanted to know where it could be found. Arnold and I had thought about going to the police with the news but decided against it. Who was going to believe us? The story even to us was a little farfetched. We didn't even know where Angel had kept the bodies, and why there was no blood or signs of force in the men's restroom of the library after the killings occurred. We didn't understand how Angel was getting away with this and why nobody had stopped him.

Although I was feeling somewhat of a connection toward Arnold romantically, he had never outright told me his sexual preference. I kind of knew he liked me though, but we just didn't do much talking about it. One thing that Angel made clear was that he could only compel and enter the minds of homosexual men. This led me to believe that Arnold may not be as comfortable with his sexuality as I was with mine. Especially since we weren't currently discussing it, but there was definitely sexual chemistry there.

One thing that made me not get too close or comfortable with the idea of being with Arnold was his current living situation. When I visited his apartment the Friday after we both met Angel for the first time, there was this guy, who was staying with him, named Carl. I assumed that this was Arnold's lover because he had a very suspicious look on his face when he was introduced to me. I kind of felt like Carl was a dog and he was marking his territory while I was there. Carl couldn't keep still, at all, while I was there at the apartment. He walked around Arnold's apartment as if he owned the place, and I felt like he was making sure I knew that as well.

I wasn't comfortable with being at the apartment, and having Carl looking me up and down, and sizing me up from the corner of his eyes. After a while of feeling the tension, I made up and excuse and left. The following day, Arnold called me after having another nightmare about Angel murdering two men at the library. I had the same dream as well, but it was too early to confirm that the murder was actually real. When I called the police station, I found out that it usually took a week or so for the Metropolitan Police Department to update their missing person's list on their website.

Arnold and I had talked on the phone every day since our first meeting. Unfortunately, with his practicing for his upcoming season and his pre-season games, we didn't have much time to see each other face-to-face. Two weeks had gone by, and I was doing my best and avoiding the restroom on the lower-level of the library like the plague. I was also trying my best to get some good sleep at night. I wasn't very successful at getting better sleep. As of late, I would toss and turn all night; too afraid to shut my eyes. When I couldn't take it anymore, and I would pass out from exhaustion, Angel would take over my dreams with killing after killing.

Arnold wanted to meet up with me today just to talk and try to find out if we could stop Angel from inhabiting one of our bodies. We also wanted to see if there was a way to get the murders to stop as well. I was very excited to see my new friend; I had wished we were meeting for different reasons, though. However, a chance to spend one-one-one time with Arnold had me jumping at the opportunity to see his handsome face again. I was never really into dark skin men, but there was something about Arnold that made him irresistible. All those late-night conversations just made me want to be with him even more. We still hadn't discussed his feelings for me. I wanted to know if it was true what Angel had said. That Arnold had followed me to the library because he was attracted to me when he saw me for the first time.

I had finally gotten my own place in an affordable apartment complex located in Hyattsville, Maryland, which was just right outside of D.C. It was a brand new building, and near the metro which made it very easy to get to work. I didn't want to go back downtown to Arnold's place and have Carl continue to give me the side eye, so I invited Arnold to my place. Of course, I suggested we go to one of the restaurants near my apartment. However, Arnold being a public figure in the area, he needed to keep a low profile. This didn't bother me much, I was just excited to see him.

I also hadn't stopped or even slowed down on my escorting. It seemed like every other day I was getting requests for dates. The money was just way too good to turn down. A lot of the men I dealt with had to keep low profiles. Therefore, I didn't mind too much when Arnold brought it up that he preferred to meet in private.

I had cleaned up my studio apartment really nice. I had the place looking more like a one bedroom, apartment than and actual studio. I had recently just purchased a room partition to separate the living space from my bedroom. I liked the way it looked, and I liked the separation of spaces as well.

When Arnold rang the buzzer, I buzzed him in and told him to come to apartment 450. I waited a few minutes and heard a light tap on my door. I opened the door to see Arnold standing there with his sparkling white teeth, looking like a sexy piece of man chocolate. Seeing Arnold standing in front of me looking good enough to eat, I had almost forgotten that I was missing the hell out of London. This even though I had just gotten off the phone with him. Yeah Arnold was something very special, to have me this excited and we hadn't even been intimate, yet.

I opened the door and said, "Come on in. I know my place is small but I'm not an all-star professional basketball player like you Mr. Man."

Arnold laughed and said, "Oh, so I am the man now? And your place is nice, so give yourself some credit. I like how you have it decorated. I should have you decorate my place. You have impeccable taste."

"Awe, you are far too kind. Please have a seat. Can I get you anything to drink? I have water, soda, juice, beer and a little bit of tequila if you are feeling naughty." I joked.

"I'll just take water and thank you so very much. You're so hospitable."

After I handed Arnold a glass of water, I fixed myself some tequila. Right before Arnold had arrived I had just entertained a client. After he came in like two seconds, I was over it. I didn't even get mine. I just thanked him for his patronage and sent him on his way. However, just thinking about the ordeal made me a little horny. I was hoping this was the day Arnold would be making his move on me.

To my delight and surprise, Arnold looked me dead in my eyes after he took his sip of water and said, "I know this is the wrong time to be starting a love affair, but I cannot stop thinking about you Pablo. I am scarred out of my mind too. I am not sure what we are going to do about Angel. Halloween is approaching and either one of us could find ourselves trapped in a world between hell and earth. I don't want that to happen to either one of us. But I am not sure if we have any control over the matter. Everything is happening all at once, and it seems so surreal. To be completely honest with you, Pablo, I've never been with a man before."

I was shocked to hear this. I pegged Arnold to be one of those down low men. I was curious, so I asked, "So what is up with you and Carl? I was for certain that the two of you were in some kind of relationship. Doesn't he live with you? When I was there he was a little cold? I felt jealously, which was why I asked you to come here today."

Arnold busted out laughing, "Oh hell no! We are just old college teammates and friends. We had a few threesomes together, but that was it. It was with women, though, and we never touched one another. I am not going to lie, before I met you I have fantasized about being with Carl. But after having him stay with me now, for over a month, there is no way in hell I want to be with someone like Carl. Carl is very selfish, and he thinks that the world owes him something. Man, if his ass wasn't hurt, I would have been kicked his ass out of my crib."

I was so very excited to hear those words come out of Arnold's mouth. I couldn't help myself, I grabbed him by the chin and brought his face closer to mine and kissed him ever so gently on the lips.

Arnold backed away at first, which shocked me. He saw the confused look on my face and he said, "It's not you at all. I've never been with a guy, let alone kissed one and it felt so good and natural. It's kind of a lot and too fast. I don't know how to take it all in."

"I'll be gentle," I said. I then took my time and worked Arnold's body like it never been worked before. He was like putty in my hands, and it was just what the doctor ordered after a lack luster client.

After I was done pleasing Arnold and myself, we'd both fell asleep next to one another, sweaty and out of breath. We both woke up the following morning and neither one of us had any nightmares. Arnold was such a nice and innocent guy. I kind of felt bad that I had my secret life of escorting. I knew he wouldn't approve of this lifestyle. Arnold was far too wholesome to understand. I wanted to be as upfront as he was with me, but for some reason I didn't have enough nerve or courage. When Arnold looked at me in my eyes I saw genuine care. Something that I had never witnessed before in anyone's eyes. I didn't want to jeopardize what we had, so I left well enough alone.

CHAPTER 12
CHAKA

I was in Pittsburgh yet again. This time I was visiting my mother. I was growing more and more impatient with this Angel demon in the men's restroom at my job. The irony of it all—how a demon could be named Angel was beyond my comprehension. Angel was more like a fallen angel if anything. I'd been back and forth to my mom's place going through my father's old things, ever since my first encounter with Angel. I was hoping to find information on how to get rid of this demon. I approached my mom as she was cleaning up her kitchen, about what I was going through at work. She tried brushing me off saying, "Chaka my dear, I left all that up to your father. I am sorry I can't be more of any help to you. I don't know much about demons and spirits. Let alone how to get rid of them."

This time though, I thought I would press the issue, because my mom seemed like she was in a more talkative mood. She still mourned my father's passing and didn't like to talk about him too often. It would put her in a very depressed state. However, somedays she would be fine discussing his memory. You just had to catch her at the right moment sometimes. I asked, "Are you sure mom? There is nothing you remember about how daddy would get rid of evil spirits? He had to have discussed at least one experience."

"Chile, when your father was alive, I was the first lady of a mega church. I would say those were the best years of my life. Unfortunately, though my duties were restricted to the annual church picnic and of course the music ministry. Everything else I left up to your father and his large staff.

"You see I was just so proud to be the first lady of his fine church. I didn't aspire to be anything other than the perfect first lady. Someone your father would be proud to have on his side. You know my grandmother was a first lady of an apostolic church, as well, when I was a young girl. It was always so nice to see her sitting next to granddaddy in the pulpit. I made it my mission to marry me a pastor myself. I was so delighted when I met your father. He and his father had visited my granddaddy's church when I was a young girl. Your dad's father, as you know was also a pastor. He spoke at the church during a revival we were having. That's what brought me and your father together for the first time, and it was love at first sight. Unfortunately, at the time your father and I were much too young to act on our feelings.

"Your daddy was so smitten by me. He told me he would come back for me and make me his first lady. He had aspirations to someday start his own church. Oh, Chaka I was only eleven years old at the time, and I waited for your daddy patiently. There were so many offers and proposals throughout the years. I held on to my virtue like granny had always taught me. I also made sure I was in church every Sunday and Wednesday. I stayed prayed up, and I sung in the choir. I was also an usher in my granddaddy's church. Anything I needed to do to snag me a preacher, I did.

"Delightfully, just as your father promised, when I was only seventeen years old, he made an honest woman out of me. Like, someday, I hope some man will do for you. Your daddy was twenty-one when he asked me to marry him. His church was a very modest size when we first got married. But, by the time he passed, I don't have to tell you, he had grown his congregation to more than seven thousand members. It was the largest black church in Pittsburgh, and boy was I a proud first lady. If granny would have lived long enough to see it, I am sure she would have been proud as well.

"Chaka, as much as I love the Lord, I am so sorry I can't be of more help to you. I wish I was more spiritually connected to God like you and your father. Honestly speaking, I never thought *that* mattered when it came to being a good first lady. I left that up to the men, and the folk that displayed those gifts. I was just happy to receive my daily blessings of good health, food on the table for my family, and a fine roof over my head. It was just an honor for me to be a part of the church that my husband presided over.

"Oh Chaka, all this talk about the church, and God is bringing back so many memories of your father, and I miss him so much. Forgive me if I need to change the subject, but feel free to take anything of your father's you need." She then left me in the kitchen alone to ponder her words.

I decided to let my mom off the hook for now. She had always been such a fragile woman. The complete opposite of the three daughters she had raised. I needed my mother now more than ever to dig deep, and to help me get rid of this demon. I knew I would be back with more questions if I couldn't figure it out on my own.

I was also visiting my hometown because my trifling tenants' final ninety days had finally expired at the end of last month. And Thankfully I had possession of my property. I was still upset that the judge had ruled in their favor, and they didn't have to pay me any of the back rent that they owed me. How it could be legal for anyone to live rent free is beyond my comprehension. I couldn't believe they were claiming that, my property was uninhabitable, but they sure lived there an additional four months after their lease had expired.

That was the least bit of my worries though. These crazy people, now that they'd moved out, were still trying to sue me for an additional thirty thousand dollars. I couldn't believe how ridiculous these clowns were being. My lawyer had the case go into arbitration since the judge wasn't really siding with me at all. I knew the judge could see that I wasn't being treated fairly, and these tenants were trying to milk their situation. It was sad that at this day and age, white privilege still prevented Blacks from getting ahead. Here I was a Black woman working to enhance the economy—I paid my taxes and invested in the economy—but I was still being penalized for renting to white folks.

My lawyer had me counter sue for the same amount, plus a dollar in hopes that the two suits would wash themselves out. My lawyer didn't think it would look good on my part if it appeared I was trying to receive any monetary compensation from my tenants. Since they were a large working class white family with a newborn and didn't have any substantial means to pay more costs to me. He put it outright, he didn't want the judge to perceive I was being a greedy Black landlord. You could be greedy and white, but definitely not greedy and Black.

I really just wanted this headache to be over, so I agreed. I was just hoping that after this last hearing I could wash my hands with these people. I had already spent more than enough time an energy on this place. I really was in Pittsburgh today in hopes to sell the property. I wanted to wash my hands of this property all together. I was putting it on the market myself, to hell with the middleman and their commissions. I planned on using my same attorney to handle the legalities, and I was well within my rights. I decided to put a sign on the front lawn with my number, and if anyone was interested all they had to do was call me.

On the upside, my budding relationship with this new guy was going great. Who would have thought Match.com was going to be able to hook a sista up like me? He agreed to drive up with me from Maryland, which I thought was nice. His name was Grant and he was in a jazz band, which I thought was exciting. Ever since I met him, I would tease him and say, "What would your groupies think of you spending so much time with me?" Grant claimed that since he "only" played the keyboard, women didn't really throw themselves at him. Unlike the lead singer, bass players, and the other members of his band. I was almost for certain that this was far from the truth, but since I had Grant's attention I didn't protest much.

I was on this new vegan kick trying to stay healthy and lose weight and get sexier for my new man. Grant seemed to not care too much about my weight. However, it was still something that I wanted to work on for personal development and just to be healthy. I'd gone vegan before and the strict diet didn't too much bother me. I enjoyed the soy protein, tofu and all the other meat substitutions. I wasn't going to lie, but after a while you just wanted a piece of chicken or a large meaty steak. That was why I quit the diet in the past, but I was trying to do my best to stick to the diet this go-around.

Since Grant ate meat and with us getting to know each other I would cook him meals that consisted of chicken, salmon, and beef. I liked Grant so much I found myself wanting to cook for him all the time. I just loved spending time with him. He was great company and we seemed to get along very well. Also, with him agreeing to come on this trip with me, he'd checked off another box on my long list of positive attributes. Supportive! It was very important to me that my man was supportive..

Grant helped to alleviate some of the stress I was going through with my rental property. The stress was literally giving me migraines. I desperately needed to get rid of the house to avoid going crazy. Nor could I deal with this demonic spirit or whatever that had taken residence at my job. I needed a break from reality and sensing this, Grant made a great suggestion, "Chaka you've been doing a lot since we got to Pittsburgh. Instead of driving all the way back to Maryland today let's check into a hotel. I'll cover the cost and give you the massage of a lifetime. Hopefully this will help you relieve some of the stress I see you're going through. You got me now. You don't have to deal with this alone, okay?"

Grant had witnessed me go through so much today. I was shocked he didn't want to just head back to Maryland and be done with me. This was a great sign that maybe, just maybe I had found the right man, for once in my life. When we got to the five-star hotel that he decided to book for the night. I was beyond impressed and thrilled. There was a Jacuzzi tub, which fit two. Grant and I had yet to be intimate. Although, I wasn't a bible toting Christian. I was raised in the church, and I tried my best not to just give the cookie away like I didn't have any home training on protecting my virtue. I also knew that men didn't really like a woman that was too easy. Even though men would sleep with a fast woman at the drop of a dime. Any man that I wanted to be with, enjoyed a challenge; so if I thought it could be serious, he had to work for the cookie.

I was also a little ashamed of how big I had gotten over the last several months. I was such a stress eater and with everything going on, I had easily gained another fifteen pounds to my already overweight body. When Grant and I got into the hotel room, we saw that there were two large white robes laying across the bed. Grant then said, "Chaka why don't you go in the bathroom and bathe. I'll be out here waiting to give you the massage of a lifetime."

Once I finished showering, I exited the bathroom with nothing on but the robe. I knew Grant didn't mind a curvaceous woman. He let it be known every time we met and over the phone. I guess he sensed my insecurities about my weight. However, even though he liked big women, that didn't mean I liked being big. Nor was I comfortable with letting a man that I liked very much, see me naked when I had gained more weight than normal. However, Grant was being persistent about seeing me naked today.

As soon as I walked out the bathroom he said, "Take off that damn robe and come here." I loved a man who knew how to take control. Being an alpha female, I could easily control a weak man. However, I followed Grant's instructions and took my robe off and laid across the bed naked as if I was on a massage table. He had cocoa butter that he'd brought with him in a duffle bag and started massaging my backside with it. His hands felt so strong and therapeutic on my body. I relaxed and let him do his thing. Grant's masculine touch pressed against my body had me in the mind of the keys he played with in his band. Every stroke and touch pressed down deep into my flesh. It sent a euphoria that only he could give me. I felt like his muse, his piano, and I treasured the feeling. His hands were magical enough that I felt it down in my groin. This immediately made my insides wet. I could feel the moisture creeping up between my legs, and I liked it. I was aroused just by his touch around my pressure points.

After I thought it couldn't feel any better, Grant flipped me on my back side with one quick swoop—I couldn't protest even if I wanted to. He then started messaging my breasts very lightly and smoothly, which only made me even wetter in my groin area. I'd never been one to get aroused just by someone's touch, but Grant must have the Midas touch. Not too much longer, I felt a finger then a tongue penetrate my insides and I just let go in ecstasy. Any and everything that weighed heavy on my mind was replaced with unimaginable pleasure.

CHAPTER 13
CURTIS

I didn't know if I should be excited or not, but London had gotten a job working at the Downtown Washington Hilton, around the corner from the library. He wanted me to start looking for a place for us to live. London wanted to be able to start his new job, as soon as possible. He was far too excited, and he was really putting the pressure on. When I first got to D.C., it took a while to get adjusted, and I was missing London something fierce. I had even contemplated moving back to Las Vegas. I couldn't believe how a few months could really change things. Now that I was here, and enjoying my freedom and being single, a relationship would kind of cramp my style. I was just starting to appreciate the move across the country, and outside of the bad dreams that

Angel was causing me, I kind of liked this new area a whole lot better than living in Las Vegas.

I really hoped that I wasn't going crazy, but Angel had to be a figment of my imagination. I didn't believe in ghosts and goblins so there was no way that this was actually happening to me. The thing that just might make me go crazy, though, didn't have to do with Angel. It was London, I never thought that he would ever decide to follow me to D.C. It's kind of bizarre actually. At one point, I did think I found the one in London, and I do love him a lot, but something just didn't feel right. It was way too sudden, and I wasn't feeling it.

While London was here visiting, he seemed very distracted, and uninterested in caring about how my new life in DC was going. He was more interested in going out to clubs, meeting up with friends that I didn't even know he had in this area. We only had sex one time, which was odd for us. Before I'd left Las Vegas, I couldn't get this nigga from up off me; but when he was here, the vibe was totally different. I didn't want to make it all about sex, but that was what London was good at, and I really did enjoy it with him.

Now that I think about it, it would had been better to see how the long-distance relationship could have worked out for us. I needed more time to see if I wanted to be so committed at such a young age. I didn't have the heart to tell London not to come to D.C. if that was what he truly wanted to do. I just wished he didn't base his decision on what I expected him to do. I'd been thinking lately of being on my own, and how would it be for me if I was self-sufficient. I still wasn't sure if I was ready for all that responsibility or could I even afford to do it all, by myself. Looking on the bright side, maybe if London was paying the other half of rent and household bills it could possibly kill two birds with one stone. I would finally be able to move out of Dr. Wilson's home.

Why not commit and do it while we're young? Who was to say that I would ever meet someone again that I felt this much in love with? I just wanted to make sure I enjoyed my youth in the process. I didn't want to grow old too fast; trying to place house. I had thought about these same things before leaving Las Vegas. I made my decision already, which was why I moved. I wasn't ready to stay in Las Vegas and play house with London. Why did this situation pop right back up again? It was a lot of pressure then and even more so now. I guess it had to be a sign that London and I were supposed to be together. Maybe the move could work, and London and I could do a lot of things I'd been doing with Pablo. As of late I'd been enjoying my stay in D.C. getting to know the area and the fun places to hang out at. Pablo was not only my co-boss, he'd also started to become one of my best friends.

We are so much alike. He was like the older brother that I never had. I will add though he was very private, unlike me I was an open book. You would never know what Pablo really had going on. The mysteriousness was killing me. I guess I was too nosey but we were getting close, and I didn't know that much about him. He, however, was a lot of fun to be around. He kept the party going. Like tonight he decided to invite me to stay at this five-star hotel in the city. Stuff like this had been going on ever since I met him. We've stayed at hotel after hotel. Sometimes the same hotel, and sometimes even the same room since we started kicking it. Things were strictly platonic between us, which I liked. Far too often gay friendships developed after the romance had died. I always felt like these types of friendships were far too complicated, because there was always one person, in the relationship, who still wished the romance would reignite.

Sometimes the hotel rooms Pablo was staying at were extremely fancy. I always thought the hotel staff was sizing us up wondering what we had going on. We were two young black guys experiencing the five-star treatment. This made me very curious about how Pablo was affording all this. In the beginning, me being the inquisitive person that I was, asked Pablo how he was affording all these rooms. He kept brushing me off or he would just say that they were complimentary rooms, but nothing more.

I wasn't born yesterday, something was up with Pablo, but I respected his privacy. If he didn't want to tell me the truth, then fine. The last time I asked Pablo, he got a little upset and rudely brushed me off again. I made a mental note that I wouldn't ever ask again. I remembered what my grandmother used to always tell me "What happens in the dark will always come to light." I was sure it wouldn't be long before whatever was going on with Pablo surfaced.

I still hadn't come to terms that Angel was really real. However, everything that had happened was too real to be fake. I just didn't know how all this was occurring. I kept thinking about when Angel said he had some information about London. I really wanted to know what information he had on London, but he would only tell me if I did him a favor. He wanted me to bring Jeffrey down to the basement of the library. I had no clue as to why he wanted Jeffrey down in the restroom. I wasn't stupid, I knew it wasn't good. I also knew I shouldn't be getting involved with Angel. There was nothing good I could even see coming from Angel, it all seemed so dark. I most definitely didn't want to go back down to that restroom, and I hadn't been back since.

Angel scared me, and if he was some sort of devil, I wanted to stay far away. As much as I didn't believe in the supernatural, I knew there was something evil and demonic about Angel. That bathroom was terrifying! I felt like I was about to die every time the lights went out. Angel would appear with his dark eyes, piercing through your body with his terrifying gaze. I was so petrified to let anyone know what I had experienced with Angel, I didn't even tell Pablo.

I knew since I didn't want to go back down there, I sure as hell didn't want to send anyone else down there. Honestly, though, no one would believe me anyway.

Angel had made it very clear that I must not mention his existence to anyone. Since I had neither come down there to see him nor done what he asked me to do, Angel had been haunting my dreams for days on end now. It had gotten so bad I was afraid to fall asleep. I kept reliving Angel's life as if I was him as a teenager, in the most compromising of situations. This morning I'd woken up out of my dream, right before I passed out from being passed around sexually by some street thugs in Angel's old neighborhood. In the dream those thugs kicked my ass so bad I just knew I was going to die in that dream. All I could hear was the thugs yelling fagot and sissy as they took turns sticking their large members into Angel's small frame. This all occurred in some back alley in the southeast part of D.C. I didn't know why Angel chose me, or if I was going insane. I did know that I was getting sick and tired of these nightmares. I felt like doing what Angel wanted me to do just to see if the nightmares would go away.
###

I had just hung the phone up with Pablo. He was calling asking me what time I was getting to the hotel tonight. Since it was Thursday night and I didn't have class the following morning, just a couple things to wrap up for school. I didn't mind going to the hotel to meet Pablo. The first thing I needed to do before close of business Friday was to turn in my paper for my English class. I had pretty much typed the entire paper today before I left school, and all I had to do was edit a few things and send it to my professor by email. Lastly, I had to take my math quiz online. I figured I could knock both of these things out at the business center at the hotel. Checkout was generally around twelvish. I knew I would be able to take care of both and be at work by two p.m.

Pablo had to be at work earlier than I did, and he never did mind me staying at the hotel until checkout. The only dilemma I had surrounding this overnight stay was my mother's new husband, Dr. Wilson. My mother was cool with me being out all night, but unfortunately Dr. Wilson didn't like it very much. My thoughts were that I was in college, doing something productive with my life. I was neither a street thug, nor out doing something I wasn't supposed to be doing. I didn't appreciate Dr. Wilson trying to manage my behavior. Besides I wasn't even his son, and I was an adult.

My mom didn't want there to be conflict between Dr. Wilson and I. Something I totally understood. She loved us both and wanted us to get along. When I told her I was leaving for the night she said, "Curtis, I really need for you to respect his house rules."

I fired back, "Isn't this your house too? Back in Las Vegas you would always let me hangout with my friends overnight, once I graduated from high school and turned eighteen. Why are you changing on me all of sudden?" I was a mommas' boy and I couldn't let no man get in between me and her. We'd been through a lot, and I her new husband needed to understand that.

My mother pleaded with me to stay once she saw my Uber out front. The Uber was here to pick me up and take me to the train station. Of course I kissed my mother on the cheek and said, "I will see you tomorrow, and I love you." I hated disappointing my mother, but she was really trying it. She needed to tell her new husband to back off and mind his business.

When I sat in the Uber, I couldn't help thinking maybe I really should give some serious thought of getting my own place. I would probably have to take out another student loan because the rent in the DMV could be pretty steep. London moving here would definitely ease the burden for me financially. I wasn't able to get a car as of yet with my refund money, because books were so damn expensive.

However, was I really ready to just settle down and be with one person? Although, I hadn't been with anyone intimately since I moved across the country other than London, that didn't mean I hadn't wanted to. I'd had some tempting opportunities that I passed up on because of this commitment that I'd made to London. We decided that we would hold out on sleeping with anyone else, until we decided that we weren't going to be together anymore. As much as I wanted to believe London was holding me in the same regard, I just wasn't so sure. Why was he so eager to move to D.C.? I wanted to believe that it was because he couldn't live without me, but something was telling me otherwise. It was mind boggling, and something just didn't feel right about his eagerness?

When I arrived at the train station there was a black Mercedes honking at me. Against my better judgment I walked over to see who was trying to flag me down. Before I could get to the car, the driver's side of the car opened, and out popped Jeffrey. Something about Jeffrey looked very appealing to me today. I wasn't sure if it was the freshly detailed luxury car or was it the physical transformation he'd undergone since the last time I saw him. Jeffery looked to be about twenty years younger, with style and swag that I hadn't recognized when I'd first met him. He looked like he had just stepped out of the best barber's chair in the area, and he smelled wonderful.

The sex appeal was undeniable, and for some reason I wanted Jeffrey or at least I thought I did. Unbeknownst to me Angel was manipulating my perception and thoughts at the moment. To the entire world, except for me, Jeffrey still looked old and washed up.

Suddenly Angel had taken control of my mind and had me seeing visions of Jeffrey's actual life. He had married his high school girlfriend after he knocked her up before they graduated. Then over the 16 years since high school, Jeffrey ended up with four more kids with this woman. He was so miserable in his marriage that it became a sport for him to lure young boys to parks, or the back seat of his car where he violently attacked them sexually.

I watched how Jeffrey would sometimes pull out knives and guns to scare his victims. He received great pleasure when he intimidated these young men. He never killed them, though, he only scared them. He then left them in abandon places, tied up but just loose enough for them to wiggle their way out of captivity. By the time his victims had gotten free, Jeffrey was long gone. Sometimes already in the house eating his wife's terrible cooking.

When the visions were done, it seemed like I was out of it for hours, but Jeffrey was still standing in front of me near his car. I then lost consciousness again, and I was in the basement of the library. Angel was in the mirror getting stronger and stronger feeding off the carnal energy of two male janitors who were performing carnal acts on each other. Something told me that this was happening this very moment and it was no flashback. How I was able to envision this was beyond my comprehension.

Angel then spoke to me in my subconscious and said, "Curtis I am getting stronger by the second now. I can almost feel your soul as if it's in front of me right now. Whatever you do, do not accept a ride from Jeffery tonight. Friday the thirteenth is tomorrow. Tell Jeffrey to meet you out in front of the library thirty minutes before it closes, and you guys both come down to see me together; and Curtis, if you know what's best for you, do not disobey me.

I snapped out of my trance and Jeffrey was still standing in front of me like nothing had just happened. I was so confused and terrified at the same time. Then I heard Jeffery say "Hey man are you okay? You kind of zoned out on me for a few seconds."

I took two deep breaths before I responded and said, "Yeah man, I am fine. I must be coming down with something, but I'll be fine. I am on my way to meet a friend, and I am kind of running late. Let me head toward the train platform."

"Which way are you headed, would you like a ride?"

As much as I would have liked to get into that car with Jeffery looking as good as he did, I decided to do what I was told. "No thank you, but I appreciate the offer. Hey before I go, what are you doing around eight-thirty tomorrow in the evening? Would you meet me in front of my job, I work at the library downtown, near Chinatown." Jeffery looked a little startled when I told him to meet me at the library, but he agreed to meet me there, nonetheless. I then boarded the next train to head to meet up with Pablo.

CHAPTER 14
ARNOLD

My life was so busy these days, I was surprised I hadn't collapsed yet from exhaustion. I guess it paid to stay healthy and physically fit all these years. The NBA season schedule was so demanding we had two to three games per week. This was a lot, especially, when you were used to only playing just one game per week. Don't get me wrong, I knew what the schedule was going to be like heading into it. Actually experiencing it was just a lot to take in. The wear and tear on my body was taking some time to get used to. I almost felt like I had arthritis some days after practice. Thankfully, Pablo was the man to the rescue. He had the firmest, yet softest touch as he rubbed my body down after many of the home games, and some of my practices. Although the team had staff on duty to take care of stuff like this, but I preferred Pablo's touch.

Carl had been extremely and annoyingly cramping my style, since he had practically moved in with me. I didn't know how long I would be able to pretend that Pablo was just a friend and a certified massaged therapist. After a few times of Pablo coming over after the games, Carl started to ask questions about who Pablo really was to me. I knew I didn't really have to explain anything to Carl. Shit I was doing him a favor by letting him crash at my apartment. However, I still wanted to keep what was going on between Pablo and me a secret. Carl was cool, but he wasn't that cool. I knew he probably couldn't handle the ideal of me being interested in another man romantically.

Last week Carl had pissed me off with some of his judgmental comments. If I had to give my reasoning behind why he even cared, I would have to say Carl was a little jealous. Why I don't know, but I had invited Pablo and his friend Curtis to my last home game. Afterwards all three of them were waiting near the player's exit for me, at the arena after the game. Of course Carl came to all the games. For some strange reason, he thought he was entitled to my complimentary tickets. The four of us started heading towards the direction of my car to head back to my place, until Carl pulled me to the side.

Something looked like it was bothering him and he finally said, "Why are we hanging out with these two? They look a little soft to me. You sure this is the type of company you want to keep? You're a professional baller now. You have to think about your reputation. We need to ditch those two. Let's go to the club and get some freaks to come back to our place."

I was so irritated by Carl's comments, he had my pressure boiling. I calmed down and said, "Our place, nigga you trippin' that's my place, and who I hang out with is my business. Pablo is cool as hell and that's his boy. You should be worrying about getting back on the court, and not who I am hanging out with."

Carl tried to laugh it off, like he was just joking and said, "Yeah they seem cool, but that Curtis dude, you need to tell him that: dudes don't wear tight jeans no more, and that the metrosexual look was never in style—only on television."

"Nigga shut the fuck up, leave those two alone, and get your high yellow ass in the car before I leave you. You should be the last one telling anybody how to dress." We all headed back to my crib for some drinks and I ordered carryout. We all chilled together and watched a few episodes of Martin, before Curtis and Carl fell asleep on the couch drunk. After seeing the two of them fast asleep in the living, Pablo and I went back to my room so I could feel those precious hands of his.

Most of time it was just easier for me to get a hotel room around the arena so I didn't have to answer to Carl. I was really close to kicking Carl out of my place. He was mad junky and he felt like he owned the place. This roommate situation had me thinking that Carl felt like I owed him something. I mean we were close in college, but I didn't remember ever having to rely on Carl for anything. What made him think he could just kick back and live the good life off of me?

Carl and I had several other team members that were doing well for themselves in the NBA. He could have easily chosen someone else besides me. What was getting on my last nerves was that Carl kept bringing women to my crib. I know he was hoping that we could relive our college glory days with partying, alcohol and group sex. Things were far more different for me now, and I wasn't the young naive country boy I used to be. Back then I was confused about my sexuality, and the things I did in the past I did to fit in. Now that I was a little older and on my own, I didn't want to have to live a lie. Nor did I have to settle for obsessing over a guy that was straight, and I could only be with was during a threesome with a woman that I had no interest in.

I didn't know how I long was going to be able to keep avoiding Carl's propositions. And to be honest I knew I shouldn't have to in my own home. Something had to give in this one-sided situation, and it wasn't going to be me being the one conceding. Today was Friday and I had an early flight tomorrow morning to Los Angeles to play the Lakers. I didn't want to put off something I could do today, tomorrow. I decided today would be the day I had that hard conversation with Carl, that I had been avoiding. Carl's sexy light skin ass was sitting on my couch, with a large bowl of cereal with his legs sprawled across the coffee table watching Wendy Williams.

I braced myself for what I knew would be a heavy conversation. I really didn't want to have this conversation with a grown ass man, but Carl wasn't getting my subtle hints. So I sat right next to Carl on my couch. I then picked up the remote control from up off the coffee table, and turned off the television. This definitely got Carl's attention because he had the nerve to raise his voice, "What the hell man? Wendy was right in the middle of her hot topics segment, and the shit was getting good. I never miss this part of the show. Turn that joint back on."

I rolled my eyes and took a deep breath before I spoke, "Carl we need to seriously talk, and I am sorry this cannot wait another day. Nor after Wendy finishes her hot topics."

Carl looked at me dumbfounded and said, "What is it that we need to talk about that is so important?"

"First we need to talk about you moving out! When I said you could crash here I never meant it to be permanent. When I picked out this apartment I didn't have you in mind, and there just isn't enough room for the both of us."

Carl started laughing like this was a joke and cut me off, "Arnold you tripping man, this big ass luxury apartment. You could fit an African village up in this bitch. You are barely even here, with your schedule. I thought I was doing you a favor by housesitting for you, and taking care of your shit."

He had got to be the dumbest nigga I knew, I thought to myself. "Carl you are sadly mistaken. I am a grown ass man and I need my space. We aren't in college anymore. I need for you to figure out what you are going to do with your life, and get off my couch. You have a lot of potential and you've been walking fine the last week or so. Don't you think you should start talking to scouts or your agent to see if you can start playing again? I know damn well you don't want to live your life in my shadow."

This must had pissed Carl off because his face went from jovial to pure dread. He started raising his voice, "Nigga are you fucking kidding me? I could never live in your weak ass shadow. I saw how you used to look at me when we was in college. You wanted to be all on this dick too. Just like all those bitches we used to fuck." Carl said grabbing his package through his basketball shorts. He continued, "See if you would have played your cards right, and not started acting like a little pussy, I was going to break you off a little piece." If I wasn't so upset I probably would have been aroused.

Carl kept going, "You think because you running around with that weak ass nigga Pablo, you don't need me. You not fooling nobody, I still see how you look at me. You still want me, don't you?"

I would had never thought in a million years, it would have gone here. I mean, I couldn't really argue with most of the accusations that Carl was throwing out. He'd really caught me off guard. I guess it didn't dawn on me or I didn't give him enough credit to think he actually knew how I really felt about him. However, I didn't appreciate his arrogance, and the way he was talking to me in my own home. I definitely wasn't about to let Carl or anyone for that matter get this best of me in my own home.

I cut Carl off. I was tired of his bullshit and I matched his tone and said, "You don't know what you're talking about. For one thing Pablo is just a friend, just like I thought we were. I don't know what has gotten into you, but I don't want anything from you, then or now. I thought I was being a good friend by helping you out during your time of need, but I guess you thought this little situation was something that it wasn't. All the more reason for you to get to stepping nigga."

Carl could see that I wasn't playing either and he calmed down a little and said, "Look Arnold, maybe I read the situation wrong, but I know when someone is into me. I've gone through people liking me all my life because of the way I look. Sometimes the looks you used to give me in college, were some of the same looks I got from women. I never acted on it because I always thought I was straight. You know I am the ladies' man out here in these streets.

"However, I was young and dumb back in college and I wasn't about to start acting on emotions that I didn't even know existed. However, when I got to Europe the men there were more aggressive than here. To be honest with you, I've experienced a few things. I want to scratch that itch for you that you've been running off with Pablo to get. Let me be there for you when you come home tired and exhausted from running up and down the court."

Carl then leaned in to me and kissed me very passionately on the lips. I jumped up from the couch, put on my jacket and said, "Look, I need to get some air, and process all of this. We can talk about this more when I get back from L.A."

"Does that mean I can stay?"

"For now."

CHAPTER 15

It was a Friday, but a particularly special Friday it was Friday the thirteenth. Whenever the thirteenth day of the month happened to fall on a Friday, demonic forces were heightened. It was like a minor Halloween to whatever was evil. Many of the evil spirits that happened to roam the earth, would receive powers they wouldn't normally possess on any regular day. This was when Angel could summon anyone he had encountered over the years to the men's lower level restroom of the library with no resistance. On these special days was when Angel did the majority of his sacrifices.

The library was quiet as usual for a Friday afternoon. Pablo was trying to keep himself busy. He wanted the day to hurry up and end, he had plans with Arnold before he left for

Los Angeles for another game. Arnold stopped going out to Pablo's apartment in Hyattsville because many of the tenants of Pablo's building started recognizing Arnold. They would stop him in the lobby begging and pleading for autographs. The last thing Arnold wanted was for anything to leak about him dating someone, let alone another man. Arnold would complain to Pablo a lot about how he'd heard so many derogatory comments his teammates had made about gay people. This made it even more frightening for Arnold to come out the closest.

Pablo had been enjoying the time he was spending with Arnold, but there was something that was bugging him about their relationship. Pablo felt like Arnold was a nice guy, but he was a little too green to the lifestyle. Pablo also felt insecure about who he really was. He thought that if he opened up to Arnold about his past and what he did on the side to make extra money, Arnold would probably not be as interested in him as he was. Pablo wasn't the type of person to put all his eggs in one basket either. He still dated other guys, and as far as the person who he was really feeling, that was London. There was something about London that Pablo couldn't put his fingers on, but it drove him crazy.

London had told Pablo last time they'd spoken that there was a huge possibility that he would be moving to D.C., and to expect to see more of him. Pablo was delighted to hear the good news. The sex between the two of them was electric, and Pablo had to admit that there had never been anyone that provided him with as much satisfaction in the bedroom as London did. Arnold was the guy you could settle down with Pablo thought, but London was the guy who rocked your world.

Pablo was in a strange mood, because he was getting really bad headaches while he was at work. He could barely get any sleep at night because Angel kept haunting him in his dreams. Pablo wasn't aware that Angel was getting stronger and his hold on Pablo was increasing by the day. Angel wanted Pablo to come down to the basement and visit him, but Pablo kept resisting. This only made Angel increasingly upset, and he would torment Pablo in his dreams. Pablo couldn't take it any longer and he decided to pay Angel a visit.

When he opened the door to the restroom he saw two men being forced inside the mirror. The two men looked to be no more than twenty years old, and all the life in their body had been sucked out of it. Angel was in the mirror with his demonic form, looking nothing like the innocent boy that appeared in Pablo's dreams. He had a look of enjoyment on his face as he increased his total number of sacrifices, pushing him one step closer to his ultimate goal. This time the lights never came on, not even for a second. Pablo could see what was happening because Angel's presence in the mirror created a red lighting effect in the small bathroom, which made the room feel even more haunted. Pablo thought to himself, *why did I come down here? This is insane. How in the hell are they getting pulled into the mirror and where are they going?*

As soon as the portal closed, and Angel's two victims were long gone, Angel directed his attention toward Pablo. "I see you been hiding from me? I already told you that you need to do what I tell you, or I am going to make your life a living hell. I feel your presence every time you enter the library, and you don't even come down to say hello. Do you know how lonely it is down here? I am sure you can imagine?"

Pablo didn't want to piss Angel off in his presence, so he said the only thing he could muster up at the moment, "I am so sorry, I've just been really busy and had a lot on my mind. I am here today aren't I?"

"You are only here because I forced you to come down here. You being down here today is not of your own free will. You aren't busy, and you can't lie to me; let's get that out of the way. This little job of yours is a cake walk. If I take your body for my own, at least I know I don't have a demanding job to go to everyday. I am sure you have a lot on your mind though, with all those tricks you been turning. I can't even blame you though, it seems like a pretty good side hustle you got going on. You're like a sex machine with all the men you allow to sample your exotic flavor. I am sure they're enjoying that Dominican pinga. I am also sure you're enjoying the power you have over these men, don't you?"

Pablo was terrified at the thought of living inside the mirror for eternity, "You don't want my life. Trust me it's not as glamorous as you think. You'd be better choosing someone better than me."

"No, you will do just fine. What did I tell you about lying? Trust me your life I am sure, is a lot better than my life was, or ever would have been."

They were suddenly interrupted by Chaka who had entered the restroom. She spoke with so much force Pablo felt a little relief, "You won't be possessing anyone's body, demon." She then looked at Pablo and said, "Get back to work. Curtis just got here, and I have something for the both of you to work on. He is in my office now getting started."

Pablo thought to himself, you don't have to tell me twice. He darted out of the restroom relieved that Chaka interrupted what was going on between he and Angel. As Pablo exited the restroom, he was hoping that Chaka would be able to live up to her promise of Angel not being able to inhabit his body. He didn't know what Chaka had under hear sleeve. However, the six months he'd been working with her, he knew Chaka meant business.

Chaka was still afraid of Angel and she didn't know if she had the power or the knowledge to defeat him. She had been reading through her father's journal all morning in hopes to find something that would help her. She thought she may have found the passages in the bible that would get rid of Angel once and for all.

When Chaka was alone in the restroom she started chanting something that she read in her father's journal that he had used once to cast out a demon from a living person. She was hoping this same passage would work on Angel. Chaka remembered the passage from Matthew chapter 12:43-45 and started chanting toward the mirror:

"When the unclean spirit has gone out of a person, it passes through waterless places seeking rest, but finds none. I will return to my house from which I came.

I will return to my house from which I came"

Chaka repeated this chant several times and for a moment Angel was caught off guard. He felt the words piercing through his lifeless flesh, almost crippling him. He wanted to retreat back into the safety confines of the mirror in hopes to rid himself of the agony. However, seconds later he began to get stronger. The *scripture* that had just immobilized him, was no longer affecting him. This was when Angel realized that on this day, Friday the thirteenth, whatever Chaka was trying to do wasn't going to work.

Angel held his ground and managed to block the anointing coming from Chaka's words from breaking his stature. He then walked out from inside the mirror, stood toe to toe with Chaka and spoke with so much fervor and ferocity that it stunned Chaka to silence. She couldn't do anything but stop her chant and listen. "Whatever you are trying to do to me isn't going to work, you fat bitch. Who do you think you are coming down in my domain interrupting me in the middle of something very important? I thought I told you to never return here or else!"

Angel used all the strength that he was able to muster up on this Friday the thirteenth, and he conjured up heavy winds. Next thing you know the doors to the restroom flew open, and Chaka was tossed out on her ass. Chaka found herself on the floor in front of the men's restroom with an injured hip from the fall. Chaka was very upset because she felt like she had failed. She didn't know what to do next, but she knew she didn't want to enter the restroom again, not now at least. Chaka was fearful of not knowing how powerful Angel really was.

Chaka went back to her office and saw Pablo and Curtis working on the guest list for the library's annual fundraiser. She politely asked them to take it into the conference room, so she could have some time to gather her thoughts on what had just happened. She wanted urgently to purge herself and the library of Angel, but she didn't know if she possessed the power to do it alone. Her father, in his journal, had made reference to a Catholic priest, by the name of Father Kind. In that journal, she read that the two of them were very close at one point in their lives. She also read several instances in which they both had defeated demonic spirits that lived on earth together.

Chaka had already placed a phone call to this man. She hadn't been able to reach him directly. Luckily, though, he was still alive and well, and was living in a monastery right outside of Baltimore. When Chaka checked her voicemail, she saw that she must had received his return call while she was away from her office. She hurried and called the private number he'd left on the voicemail, and to her surprise the phone picked up in one ring.

"Thank you so much for returning my call. I'd read so many good things about you in my father's journal. I am so glad we are getting a chance to speak." Chaka said through the phone connection.

Father Kind replied, "After all these years, I finally get to talk to the apple of my dearest friend's eyes. To what do I owe this honor?"

"Father Kind I wish it was for another reason, but I need your assistance. You see I've been experiencing paranormal activity at my workplace. It appears to be of the demonic kind, and it's pretty powerful. Today I tried reciting a phrase from the Bible my father once used to ward off evil spirits, and it didn't work for me."

"Well depending on what passage you used, you will have an uphill battle trying to perform any religious ritual on Friday the thirteenth. This is one of the days the devil's power is heightened. You will have to be very specific when it comes to these evil spirits, on this day in particular. Depending on how powerful this spirit really is will also determine what ritual will vanquish him. You also have to know what exactly you are dealing with. There isn't one passage for all demonic spirits unfortunately. I am pretty busy this week and part of next week, but I am more than willing to assist you. Your father once told me that you inherited his foresight and gifts. I am sure whatever it is, you will be able to get rid of it just hold tight for a bit."

Chaka felt a little better after her conversation with Father Kind. She just hoped that he got back with her sooner than later, before Angel was able to harm anyone else. Chaka then went to the conference room, so she could speak to Pablo about what she'd overheard between him and Angel's exchange.

Pablo and Curtis were working diligently on their task when Chaka interrupted them and asked to speak with Pablo alone in her office. Curtis was hoping that nothing bad was going on with Pablo since they were really hitting it off. Pablo was like the fun older brother that Curtis always wished he'd had. They had just spent last night drinking, gossiping, and listening to music at a five-star hotel. Curtis was still very curious to know how Pablo was able to book all these fancy rooms.

Curtis knew that Pablo sometimes stayed in hotels with Arnold, when the Wizards played a home game. So, since Arnold was on the road most of the time, Curtis couldn't explain how Pablo still had access to the five-star hotel rooms. Even still, Curtis tried not to pry. He just wanted to know what was going on. He'd hoped that nothing illegal was going on because he didn't want to be there when the cops raided the place. However, Curtis gave his new friend the benefit of the doubt because they were having such a great time hanging out. It was hard to make new friends in a new city. Curtis felt like the few gays that he encountered were very cliquish. So, he welcomed the time spent with Pablo.

###

After Curtis wrapped up the guest list, he did his daily tasks until it was almost closing time. He received a text from Jeffrey letting him know he was out front of the library waiting on him. Curtis thought to himself, *what am I getting myself into?* Angel had left Curtis alone the previous night, so thankfully he didn't have any nightmares. This made Curtis all the more excited to hopefully do this one last thing for Angel, and be done with him for good.

Curtis texted Jeffrey back and told him to meet him in the basement in the men's restroom in five minutes. Curtis didn't want any of the security guards, or any of his co-workers to see him walking a customer to the restroom. When Jeffrey read the text from Curtis he thought it was odd that Curtis wanted to meet in the restroom. Jeffrey had history in that particular restroom. At first he hesitated, not having been back since that frightful day, sixteen years ago, when he'd gotten out of hand and accidently murdered Angel, the pretty effeminate boy from homeroom his senior year.

He was hoping there wasn't any funny business going on. The only reason why he even agreed to meeting Curtis at the library was because, *there was no way of Curtis knowing what had happened*, he thought. Curtis was only a baby at the time, and he wasn't even from the area. Jeffrey remembered that Angel's body was never found, and that the police instead of ruling it a homicide, concluded that Angel must had just ran away. The police had talked to a lot of Angel's teachers and friends, and everyone gave statements that Angel was a troubled teenager and felt like he didn't belong.

The closing of Angel's case put Jeffrey a little more at ease when he decided he wanted to take Curtis up on his offer. Jeffrey was very much attracted and interested in Curtis ever since he'd laid eyes on him. He really wanted to get Curtis alone; and now, he finally had the chance. When Curtis entered the men's restroom, the lights were off and nobody was in there. Soon as he made his first step into the bathroom the motion lights flickered on, and moments later Jeffrey waltzed into the restroom.

It appeared that the two of them where alone, Jeffery had assumed. He had no clue Angel was inside the mirror watching his every move. Jeffrey started flirting with Curtis, "You're looking extremely handsome today. You have the cutest little frame, with a remarkable ass. I love slim guys with juicy butts like yours. Do you like getting your ass ate? I want you to sit on my face and let me see if I can get rid of this hunger I had all day."

Curtis blushed, but he was too frightened to even get aroused. He was wondering why Angel hadn't appeared yet. He'd done what he was told, and he wanted to move on with his life. Jeffrey had thought something sexual and carnal was going to happen between the two of them. However, Curtis although he was still seeing Jeffrey in a different manner than he appeared to everyone else. He couldn't get the fear of Angel out of his mind to even think about performing any sexual acts with Jeffrey in this restroom. Besides, Curtis was not the type of person to perform sexual acts in a public setting; let alone where he worked. He also was still trying his hardest to keep his promise to London and refrain from any sexual contact while they were apart.

Jeffrey not understanding why Curtis was being so shy and quiet asked, "You asked me to meet you down here didn't you? Why you acting so damn shy? Say something, or you just want me to undress you right here and now?"

Before Curtis could protest, the lights went dark and suddenly Angel appeared in the mirror. Angel was in his human form and looked the same as he did when Jeffrey left him there to die. Angel was angry enough to transform into his demonic form at the sight of Jeffrey, but he wanted Jeffrey to know who he was dealing with.

Angel then spoke through the mirror, piercing through Jeffrey's weathered life form and said, "Not so fast motherfucker. As much as I probably would enjoy watching the two of you get it on in front of me. Unfortunately for you Jeffrey your fun comes to an end today."

Jeffrey thought that he was imagining things. He knew he'd murdered Angel in cold blood, right here in this very bathroom. He looked toward Curtis for moral support, but Curtis stood in the corner shrieking in fear. Angel then changed from his young mortal self to the demon he had turned into. Jeffrey was dumbfounded, and he wanted answers.

He started talking to Angel through the mirror, "How could this be possible, you're supposed to be dead? What are you? Who are you and why am I here?"

Angel laughed, "Yeah it's me, Angel. You're right you did try to kill me all those years, but as you can see you weren't very successful. A witch with extraordinary power was visiting the library that tragic day. She heard my cries that you tried to silence. She got to me right before the last breath had left my body. Unfortunately, she didn't have the power to bring me all the way back to life. That is something I am going to have to do for myself, and by killing you, puts me one step closer to getting out of this damn mirror."

Angel didn't waste any time in levitating Jeffery towards the mirror and sucking him inside. Within seconds, there was no trace that Jeffery had ever entered the restroom. Curtis sat in the corner watching in terror. He was hoping and praying that he wasn't next.

As soon as Jeffrey disappeared through the mirror Angel focused his attention on Curtis. "You did good work, today Curtis. Thank you for bringing me my tormentor so I could impose his final judgment. The world has seen the last of Jeffrey Lance, and the world will now be a better place. I told you that I would give you some information about your lover, London, didn't I?" Curtis had totally forgot all about what Angel had to tell him about London, after baring witness to Jeffery's demise. Curtis stood there still in shock, but very focused on what Angel had to reveal to him.

Angel continued, "Those closest to you cannot be trusted. Be very mindful of the new people you allow into your life. Pablo isn't the friend that you think he is. He's a selfish, narcissistic, sex addict. He and London have been messing around behind your back. I hate to be the bearer of bad news, but I thought you should know who you are dealing with. For what you did for me today, I will no longer bother you. You are free to go."

Curtis walked out of the bathroom with a bittersweet feeling resonating from his thoughts. He didn't know if he wanted to go to the conference room and curse Pablo out or get on his phone and call London and rip him a new one. When he got to the lobby of the library he saw a familiar face walking inside, it was Arnold. Arnold had just left his apartment after getting into a heated argument with Carl about moving out. Carl had revealed something that he wasn't ready to deal with, so he left in a hurry.

Arnold didn't want to step foot in the library again, but he didn't have anywhere else to go, and he really wanted to see Pablo. Arnold, watched Curtis rush passed him without saying a word. The "don't fuck with me" look on Curtis' face, made Arnold turn the other way. He didn't know what was going on with Curtis, but he knew better and left well enough alone.

Arnold checked his phone and he saw the text coming from Pablo saying that he would be ready to go shortly. He just had to finish up something. While Arnold was waiting in the Lobby for Pablo to get off, he got the urge to go down to the lower level men's restroom. As much as he didn't want to see Angel, he felt he should face his fears. Arnold didn't have a clue that he didn't have any control of the matter, and Angel was using his powers to lure Arnold back down to the restroom. When Arnold entered the restroom, the lights popped on and then off. Angel didn't waste any time coming to the mirror.

Angel spoke up and said, "Finally after all these months I finally get to see you again, face-to-face. I know you're off becoming this huge basketball star, something I look very forward to myself. You know after the more I think about it, your life probably would be more interesting than Pablo's life. At least I'll be around sexy, hot, tall men, with perfect physiques. I bet you love those locker room visits, don't you?"

Arnold was not in the mood for Angel's fun and games, "Look, why do you continue to haunt my dreams? This has gone on long enough. It's affecting my sleep and my game. Who the hell are you, and what can I give you besides taking over my life to make all this go away?"

Angel laughed, "That's all you can do for me, but in the meantime, you can continue to come down and visit me.

It gets lonely down here, and you're an attractive guy; I would love to spend more time getting to know you. Especially if I am going to be you someday soon."

"You've got to be kidding me if you think I am going to spend my time talking to a dead guy in a mirror. Do whatever you think you can do inside that mirror, but you will not get any help from me." Arnold walked out the restroom and back upstairs to the lobby of the library. He could hear Angel's devilish laugh as he stormed out.

Luckily when Arnold got back upstairs Pablo was in the lobby waiting for him. Pablo asked, "Please don't tell me you went back down there where Angel is?"

Shaking his head Arnold answered, "Yes, but I wish I never stepped foot in that restroom. This is so bizarre! What's happening down there, there has to be a way for us to stop this and quickly."

"Well you may not have to worry much longer. My boss, Chaka, she is some sort of prophet or something. She assured me she knows what to do to get rid of Angel and for good. She just told me today that I don't have to worry much longer about Angel."

"Are you serious? Your boss knows what's going on down there? Who told her?

"I am not sure how she knows, but if I know her she has everything under control."

"Well it doesn't look that way, but I guess I will hope for the best. Hey, I just saw Curtis not too long ago. He looked very upset is everything okay between the two of you? He walked passed me and didn't say a word"

"Yeah everything is fine. You know we just hung out last night. I am sure it's nothing. I haven't really talked to him since earlier, though. He was missing in action toward the end of the day. However, I am sure everything is okay I will catch up with him tomorrow, while you're off in L.A.

trying to win another game. Today, I want to focus my attention on you and you alone.

CHAPTER 16
PABLO

Arnold was making this very difficult for me to not fall in love with him. While he was in town, and not on the road, he showered me with attention, nice gifts, and good dick. He was, however, a little too gentle for my liking, when it came to sex. I wished he was a little rougher with me, not all the time, but most of the time. I wanted Arnold to choke me sometimes, bite the hell out of my nipples instead of just kissing them, or even slap me around like a rag doll. In the bedroom he was way too sensual and loving. I felt like I was too much for him at times. I was sure if he found out about my past he would surely runaway.

London had moved into town and he was staying at a rooming house in Columbia Heights until he found something permanent. He would stay a few nights at my place during the week, but London was too busy enjoying what D.C. had to offer. This didn't matter to me much, because I had my clientele and of course Arnold when he was home. I wasn't mad at London for keeping his options open. Especially considering all that I had going on, but I did wish Arnold could match London's sexual ferocity in the bedroom. Maybe just maybe I would try and settle down and try to give Arnold what he's been giving me, exclusivity.

Arnold was starting to pressure me about my past life. It didn't surprise me that the fact that I had gone to the Olympics came up. One time we were talking about my physique and he was asking me why I was so athletic. He said, "Pablo, I swear you must have ran track or something, because your body is just too lean and tight to not have played any sports. I know an athletic body when I see one." I was really getting comfortable with Arnold, and over drinks it slipped out. I accidently told him that I'd ran track, and I'd even made it to the Olympics for my country. This had definitely slid out my mouth way too quickly, because I was not in willing to divulge my deepest darkest secrets.

There were certain things that I wanted to go to my grave with. As much as Arnold seemed head over heels over me. I knew this was all new to him. He needed more experience in this lifestyle. Most of all he needed to date more guys. The last thing I wanted to hear was five years down the road, he ended up meeting someone that was more of his soul mate than I could ever be.

Although, I was enjoying residing in the D.C. area and getting to know new people, this Angel demon was still a pain in my ass. He was so fucking annoying and scary. I thought Chaka would have taken care of him by now, but she admitted to me that it was more challenging that she had first thought. This only made me even more frightened for my life. I tried to keep myself busy, and not focus too much on the negativity. However, Angel was not loosening his grip on me.

I felt like he wanted me to suffer until he was able to take possession of Arnold's or my body. I, however, was going to do everything in my power to make sure this didn't happen to me. I didn't want to lose Arnold either, but better him than me. I knew this sounded very selfish, especially since I had feelings for Arnold. Hell, I wish he could just find someone else to torment instead of us. Why did I have to be the unlucky person to fall prey to this paranormal thing?

Also, things had been weird between Curtis and myself. I wasn't sure why he'd been giving me the cold shoulder all of a sudden. I knew that I was having sex with London, behind his back, but I was almost certain he hadn't figured it out. When I found out about London being Curtis' boo, I did feel bad, but I was too far deep in lust. London and I, had been very discreet. We both knew that it would be for Curtis' best interest that he didn't find out. Curtis was very young and impressionable, having come from a very caring and loving background. Both London and I didn't have the heart to hurt Curtis and tell him what was going on. I missed Curtis and our constant work chatter, and our evening gatherings. I had just thought I may have found my best fucking friend for life, but now he was so distant, and I didn't know why.

Today was a special day for me. I had a date with one of my richest clients. I was told by Coach Diego that this guy was close to being a billionaire when I'd met him when I was still in high school. He was the main reason I'd gotten kicked off my countries Olympic team. His name was Jean Sutherland, and he was a former Olympic Gold medalist, from Great Britain. When I'd met him when I was sixteen; he'd just started making his fortune as a venture capitalist. He had taking his endorsement money from winning the gold model in the decathlon and made some pretty wise investment decisions.

Back when I lived on the island, Jean would come see me almost every month once his money started to make money. Jean had a wife and three kids that resided in London, England. He would always talk about how he wished he could just stay on my island for the rest of his life and be with me. I wasn't very attracted to Jean. He was a little too needy for me; but he had achieved the dream that I wanted for myself—my very own gold medal. I was a little more intrigued by him, than I normally would have been had he not been an Olympian. After a while, I kind of started enjoying spending time with him and hearing his advice.

The fiasco of me getting kicked off my country's Olympic team, coupled with Jean's little-to-no-contact with me during and directly proceeding that horrendous experience, had me upset with him. He was part to blame but tried to keep his hands clean and reputation intact. I had been seen leaving Jean's hotel room during the 2016 Olympic Games that were being held in Brazil. I was slated to compete in two events, the 110 meter hurdles and the 400 meter hurdles. Jean was an official for the Olympic Games that same year and me being seen leaving his room was a violation of the International Olympic Committee rules.

Unfortunately, the alternate that my country sent with me was a very jealous person. His name was Alejandro and he wanted his shot to compete in the Olympics; however, I was much faster and secured the only spot. He was a lot slower than me and ended up placing last in both races at the Olympics he stole from me. Why he snitched on me and jeopardized our country's only chance at winning a gold medal was beyond my comprehension. However, the fact that he placed dead last was what he'd gotten for not being a team player, and a snitch.

After Alejandro snitched on me it, was decided that I couldn't compete. I had to leave Brazil immediately and go back to the Dominican Republic. I lost all my sponsors and potential endorsements for winning the gold. My life was ruined, and Jean was nowhere to be found. The only number I had for Jean was never answered, and none of my phone calls were returned until just a few days ago. Not too long ago, I had gotten a call from Coach Diego saying that Jean had come to the island looking for me. He said that Jean felt terrible and wanted to help me out in any way that he could. At first, I was hell bent on paying Jean dust. I had happily bounced back and moved on with my life. If I played my cards right I could become a permanent resident or even a citizen of one of the richest countries in the world—the United States of America. My boss Chaka had already told me that she planned on promoting me after a year of working at the library. I was more than good now.

Then I came to my senses and thought what the hell, Jean was always nice to me. It wouldn't hurt to at least see what he had to say to me. When I called him two days ago, he'd said that he was coming to D.C. for a meeting and that he would love to see me. I agreed to meet with him and he was staying at The Hyatt Washington, D.C., which was close to the library. I was leaving work now to head over to meet Jean. He wanted to meet in the hotel restaurant for drinks, and I needed a drink badly.

When I arrived at the restaurant, Jean was sitting at the bar and I greeted him. He then said, "America, the land of the free looks good on you. I see you picked up a few pounds. It's really good to see you. I reserved us a table. I was just waiting for you to come in, you know I hate eating alone." Within seconds we both got escorted to a cozy table for two. We sat near the window, so we could view the city and passersby if we wanted.

When we sat down, Jean started talking again, "Let me first tell you how sorry I am that your dreams were suddenly stripped away from you, all because of me. I didn't know the rules fully before I asked you to come to my room in Rio. You could have won a medal that summer, and it's all my fault. Life for you now would be so much different if it weren't for me."

As much as I enjoyed Jean taking on the blame and apologizing, I really couldn't put it all on him. However, I wasn't going to share in the blame in front of Jean though. So, I said, "Yeah it was really rough for me following the events that occurred after the Rio Olympic Games. I thought my life was over. I even contemplated suicide. If it wasn't for the opportunity to come to the United States, I don't know what would have become of me."

"I am also so very sorry that I kind of left you out to dry. I was so embarrassed by the accusations that were flying around about me. I didn't even think about what sort of position this would have put you in either. I was more so trying to protect my reputation and family."

I was glad he touched on that because this was what really bothered me. So, I responded, "That was what bothered me the most. Prior to the debacle, you had always acted like you cared about me. That I was more to you than a prostitute. However, when things got too hot in the kitchen, you just left me to fend for myself. Jean, that's why it's so hard for me to accept your apology."

Jean was in tears by this point. I wasn't sure if he was being sincere or not but shit I should be the one crying not him. He continued with his conversation through his tears. "Pablo, you have to understand I do care about you that is why I am here now. Trying to make those past wrongs into right. Is there anything that I can do for you that would allow us to get back to where we were?"

"Jean you know I haven't really given it much thought to be honest. Maybe there is something that you can do for me. Let me think long, and hard about this and get back to you."

Jean started to perk up once he realized that there could possibly be something between us again. I also remembered that he always paid well, and my current salary at the library was very modest. So, after drinks and dinner, I was more than willing to go upstairs today, and supplement my income the best way I knew how.

CHAPTER 17
CHAKA

I finally got an offer on my rental property back in Pittsburgh. This was a bittersweet moment for me. I would finally be letting this property go. I had it for almost ten years; and when I first purchased it, I had thought I would have it for the rest of my life or at least until I received an offer that I couldn't refuse. However, since it was costing me more money to maintain it than I was actually profiting, it was time to get rid of the liability.

My tenants from hell had finally moved out, which I thought would never happen. They still were trying to sue me though; and now that I have an offer for the house, they thought they could block the sale. Maybe they thought I would be desperate enough to settle the case and give them what they were asking for. I did however, offer them a $1,000 settlement, just so I could be done with them. Unfortunately, they didn't accept my offer. They thought they were going to squeeze more money out of me. My lawyer assured me that I would be fine and ready to settle on my rental property in thirty-days. Due to the pending status of the case, they had no right to block the sell or put a lien on the property.

I was so glad to hear this, because these fools were really trying to drive me to drinking. I still didn't know why they thought I owed them anything when they lived several months in my house rent free. However, I could only assume that when you didn't have very much to work with, some folks tried to get it anyway they could; even if it meant lying and stealing from others. These people knew they were dead wrong, but at the end of the day they were wasting their time and money because I was more than accommodating to this family.

I had way too much on my plate at the moment. I had just been elected as the president of my homeowners' association. I thought this new responsibility would be a cake walk; boy, was I wrong. When looking through the books I noticed that the previous president had been stealing from the association. The homeowners association's bank account only had five hundred dollars in it. I knew something had to be wrong, there should have been ten times that amount in the bank account. I couldn't believe that this man was robbing the very own community he lived in.

Not to mention with my busy schedule; it has been days since I'd talked to Father Kind. Angel was a thorn in my side, and I wanted nothing more than to get rid of him for good. When I did talk to Father Kind, he told me if I could see Angel, then I could defeat him. Father Kind had visited me at the library a week and a half after I first reached out to him. However, when I took him down the lower level men's restroom, Angel had the nerve to not come out.

The following day I went down there alone and of course Angel came out to threaten me. He warned me that if I didn't leave him alone, he would kill me. He also warned me to never bring back Father Kind. When I spoke to Father Kind about this threat, he reassured me that Angel didn't have the power to kill someone as powerful as myself, and if he could have he would have done so already.

I remember Father Kind saying, "Evil isn't tough or powerful, nor can it defeat good. Evil preys on the weak, and on the nonbeliever because it knows their strength is limited. The paranormal creature's main goal is to become normal, human again. It's not an easy feat for them, but the weak minded make it easier for these spirits to reach their goals, because they are afraid. The weak and the nonbeliever will do whatever evil wants them to do."

Father Kind's words put a little bit of solace in my heart. However, I wanted to protect those who couldn't help themselves, like Pablo. As much as I liked Pablo, I had a feeling that Angel had gotten to him. There was no telling what Angel had planned for Pablo or anyone who went into that bathroom. Apparently, unexplained disappearances had be occurring for years at the library. I had done my research, and when reading some of the missing persons' reports all the victims were young men. They were all seen visiting the library on the days they were reported missing. I couldn't help but wonder if Angel had something to do with every single missing person.

What I also found, was a missing person's report that fit the description of Angel. Angel Ramirez was last seen headed to the library more than sixteen years ago. Father Kind wanted me to uncover everything we could find out about Angel, and what happened to him would help us in getting rid of him. My powers were starting to get stronger as well. I had a dream the night before and in this dream, I saw the death of Angel in that same bathroom where he hid inside the mirror. I also saw a witch sitting on the third floor of the library, who was able to sense the attack as it was happening. After the attack, I saw this same witch as clear as day, enter the restroom where Angel laid, beaten, bruised, and almost lifeless.

I couldn't make out what she was chanting, but I saw Angel's remains disappear from the floor, there was no trace of his body or blood. Then, within seconds you could see him trapped inside the mirror, begging the witch to let him out. Then I was suddenly awaken from this dream. I had been replaying what I dreamt about in my head for the last several days. Trying desperately to piece everything together in an attempt to get rid of Angel.

I hadn't been able to reach Father Kind to explain to him that I had some sort of premonition. I kept searching for answers out of my father's journal, and kept coming up empty handed. I had almost reached the end of his journal and I was frustrated that nothing had come up that would help me get closer to vanquishing Angel. In a few minutes I had dinner plans with Grant. Grant had been asking me for weeks what had gotten into me. He noticed a change and he wanted to know what was up. I continued to assure him that it was nothing that he'd done.

Grant had actually kept me sane during this crazy period in my life. Not to mention he was the consummate lover. Even though I was sinning by having sex with Grant, I knew he was the man for me. I contemplated talking to him about stopping our sexual activity until we got married. I hadn't talk to Father Kind yet, but I kept feeling guilty about my practice of premarital sex. I was wondering if the reason I couldn't cast out this demon from the library, was because I wasn't living a Holy life, like my father always had. When reading my father's deepest darkest secrets, he often talked about his gifts not being as strong when he was struggling with sins of the flesh.

I didn't want to lose Grant and I knew sex was a big part of our relationship ever since we started having it. He was just like any other man, he wanted it all the time. I enjoyed it as much if not more than he did, so I never turned him down. However, I did feel guilty afterwards because he hadn't made me an honest woman. I wasn't raised to just play house with men. I was raised to become some man's wife. It was about time I started acting like the woman I was raised to be and be up front with Grant.

Grant picked me up and took me to my favorite vegan restaurant, Trufood Kitchen in Fairfax, Virginia. This man was the epitome of thoughtful. Grant was far from a vegan, but he didn't mind eating like one for me. When we sat down at the restaurant, Grant started in like he normally did, "I know you're trying to get small with all this healthy eating. Just don't get too damn small. I like laying up against something. No boney women for me, no sir no ma'am." He then laughed.

I guess since I didn't laugh with him he thought I was upset at what he just said, "Baby you know I am just joking right. You know I'll love you any size or shape you are comfortable in."

This was the first time I heard him say he loved me. I was smitten at the fact that he finally said it, because I had already fallen in love with Grant. The first night we made love in that five-star hotel in Pittsburgh, he'd stolen my heart. However, let's just hope he felt the same way after I had this serious conversation we were about to have. I assured him, "Grant I have nothing to be upset about. I love that you love the way I look. Hell, you love my body more than I do. Your comments about loving my size always makes me feel good inside, you don't ever need to worry about that.

"However, this is the first time I believe I heard you say that you loved me. That is why I got quiet on you. So, you really love me?"

Grant smiled, laughed and said, "Chaka you are an incredible woman. I would be a fool not to fall in love with you. You are the perfect woman for me." I thought to myself, *then why haven't you asked me to marry you? Why are you just telling me you love me? Why don't you make an honest woman out of me, so I can stop feeling so guilty?* He continued, "Not to mention, you have the best pussy I've ever had in my life."

I cringed when I heard that, and I couldn't believe he was admitting that to me. I interrupted him, "Let me cut you off before you go any further. You know my father was a pastor, and I was raised with certain values. I am a proud Black woman, but I am not perfect. I kind of let a lot of my values go in an effort to make you happy. Hearing you say that you love me, I appreciate you finally admitting that, but actions speak louder than words. Every time I make love to you I feel guilty afterwards because you aren't my husband.

"Although I don't go to church every Sunday, I am a very spiritual woman. I don't want you to think that I am crazy because I am not. Basically, I have been given special gifts from God. Gifts that not very many people can brag about possessing."

Grant was looking at me with a shocked look on his face and said, "Damn baby, I knew you was a special woman, but special gifts from God. What are you basically trying to tell me, because I am sitting here lost as a motherfucka?"

I knew this would be a difficult conversation, but if Grant was the one he needed to know everything. I spent about an hour explaining to him everything that was going on at the library. I came clean about Angel and how Father Kind had been helping me tap into my gifts. I also revealed that he and I wouldn't be partaking in premarital sex any longer. We ended the night with Grant letting me know that he needed time to process everything, which I totally understood. However, it didn't stop the tears that came from my eyes once I got in my bed alone.

CHAPTER 18
CURTIS

I couldn't stop thinking about Jeffrey and how I helped strip a father away from his family. A week after his disappearance, I saw his wife on the nightly news crying, pleading for anyone to step forward with any news on her husband's whereabouts. Jeffrey's wife looked so pitiful with her young children clinging to her disheveled body as she spoke into the camera. I didn't know what was worse; not being able to sleep because of Angel's nightmares or the guilt I was feeling.

I had decided on not moving out of Dr. Wilson's home after I heard Angel's revelation about London and Pablo. I wasn't about to jump into a relationship with someone who would try and deceive me. However, this didn't stop London from moving to D.C. He made that move without my support or blessing. I guessed he really wanted to be closer to Pablo, but little did he know Pablo was just as deceitful as he was. Pablo and London deserved each other, but I was sure it wouldn't work out between them. Pablo would be stupid if he chose London over his NBA player boyfriend, Arnold.

I had decided that I wouldn't make a scene or even acknowledge that I knew what was going on between the two of them, right away. I was hurt, don't get me wrong. I did, however, want both of them to know that I knew what was going on. However, I hadn't decided yet, what I was going to do about it. Apparently, London had found his way to the lower level of the restroom of the library and had been acquainted with Angel himself. I wouldn't be surprised if Angel had compelled London to move all this way.

Before I walked out that restroom for good, Angel told me that if I wanted revenge I could help him possess either Pablo or London's body, so he could finally escape his prison sentence inside the mirror. Angel said that he didn't really need my help, and that he was more than capable completing this undertaking. He thought that after hearing what was being done to me, that I may want to get my hands dirty once again. Angel was mistaken, though, I wasn't getting back in bed with the devil ever again.

I wasn't sure what I was going to do or how I wanted to get back at those two; and after seeing what had become of Jeffrey, I didn't want to have to deal with Angel ever again. I believed in God, and that Jesus was my Lord and Savior. I didn't know exactly what Angel was, but I did know he was far from angelic. I didn't want to mess around, and accidently give my soul over to the devil, just because I had been heart-broken and deceived by a person who I thought was a friend.

London had been blowing up my phone for weeks since he'd moved. I kept avoiding him; giving him excuse after excuse why I couldn't meet up with him. I received a long text from him today that read:

I miss you a lot Curtis. You know you are my heart. Why are you avoiding me? What could I have possibly done to you to get this type of treatment? I would have never expected you of all people would treat me like this. Pick up your phone when I call you or call me back. I been in D.C. for over a month and have yet to see you. Don't you want to see me? I moved here to be with you and I understand if you aren't ready for a huge commitment, but to just ignore me. I don't know how much more I can take of this. Please call me.

I thought it was funny how he was asking me what he'd done. He should have known that he couldn't get away with cheating on someone. Even if Angel hadn't told me, I would have still figured it out. Shit, I had already known something was different when he came to visit. I had moved on from London finally, so he was short if he thought we were getting back together. There was this guy name Jabari in my Spanish class who I had went to the movies with, and out to eat a few times since learning that London was a cheater.

Jabari had been asking me out since the first day of class, but I thought he was too old for me and I was trying to be committed to London. Jabari had just turned thirty. He was a D.C. native and was laid off from his job. Fortunately for Jabari, he'd received a generous severance package that allowed him to go back to school and get his degree free of charge. Jabari seemed to be a very good person thus far. He was a little rough around the edges, but he was definitely good looking.

I had never been to Jabari's home before and he invited me over to his place tonight, so we could do the whole Netflix and chill thing. I hadn't stayed out all night since I stopped hanging with Pablo. My mother and especially Dr.

Wilson were elated that I was coming home every night. My relationship with Dr. Wilson had actually improved a great deal since the betrayal. We started spending one-on-one time together, and getting to know each other. Just the other day, he took me to the new MGM casino that had opened up not too far from where we lived at the National Harbor.

Dr. Wilson had explained to me how he was sorry if he was hard on me, and how he appreciated my recent efforts regarding his house rules. This conversation only made me feel worse, because Dr. Wilson didn't know that I was only home because of circumstance, not because I was obeying his house rules. However, I just listened and enjoyed getting to know my mother's new husband.

I hoped when I left out the house tonight, that things wouldn't go back to how they were, and we could remain tension free. I had been in such a bad mood lately. I kind of welcomed Jabari's eagerness in wanting to get know me. Jabari made me feel wanted and appreciated after London's deceitful ass. It was hard not feel a little inferior to Pablo, since he was from another country. For some reason the Latin culture, especially Dominicans were the craze right now in America. I didn't want to think about having low self-esteem, but it was hard when you put me up against Pablo.

Jabari picked me up on time, at eight o'clock in the evening. I was happy because Dr. Wilson and my mother had gone out for a movie, so they weren't home when I left. I did, however, send my mother a text letting her know not to expect me home tonight.

When we arrived at Jabari's place, I was pleasantly surprised that he owned his own Townhome in Southwest D.C. It was not too far from the Eastover Shopping Center, and I had been there before shopping. Jabari had two small dogs that rushed to the door as soon as we walked inside. They started barking once they noticed a stranger was entering their home.

Jabari told the dogs to move and be quiet as we entered the home. He also said to me, "Don't mind these two. They aren't used to seeing visitors. You are the first guy that I brought to my house since my divorce."

Jabari hadn't spoken to me regarding his past, so I was a little shocked to find out he used to be married, so I pried, "Oh you've been married before?"

"Yes," he replied. "I married my high school sweetheart, and we had a child together right after high school. We divorced about a year ago. She moved to Georgia for her job, and my son moved with her. He was here over the summer, though."

"Oh ok, so are you bisexual," I asked.

"Oh no, not at all. I have been hiding from my sexuality for a very long time. I thought I could ignore it, but that was me being immature. I couldn't deny my natural feelings; and as a result, my marriage was suffering. My ex-wife and I are still friends, but I know I hurt her in the process."

I tried to comfort Jabari, since he obviously had a hard time talking about this. "Well at least you didn't live your whole life living a lie. I am also glad that I got a chance to meet you because you are a very special guy. Enough of this serious talk. Let's watch that new Will Smith movie Bright on Netflix. I heard that it was really good."

The two of us got cozy on his couch in the basement where he had a wide screen, HD television on the wall. It looked like a very nice place to watch the Super Bowl, or the NBA playoff games. Instead of us watching the movie, it ended up watching us. Fifteen minutes into the movie I felt someone's hand trying to find its way down my pants.

When I turned my head from the television towards Jabari his lips gently touched mines. Then I felt his tongue parting my lips and opening them up to get inside my mouth. Once his tongue touched mine, I got all woozy inside and decided to let go of my nervous energy. At this point I was down for whatever. It had been months since London and I hooked up, and my body needed some attention.

Once Jabari's hands found themselves inside my pants, he undressed me right there on his couch. I laid their naked with his hands and tongue touching me on all the places that I loved. Jabari was very aggressive and moved quickly, but sensual. Every touch was magnetic, and I couldn't help but whimper in ecstasy as he explored every inch of my body. The difference between him and London was that Jabari was passionate about pleasing me. Not that London wasn't in the pleasing department. London was more so interested in pleasing you in one way, and one way only. It consisted of him sticking his gigantic meat inside you, until you couldn't do anything but climax in pleasure-filled pain.

In contrast, Jabari's techniques were very romantic and calculating. He knew the pleasure points of the body. I swore I could climax with no penetration whatsoever, but that wasn't something Jabari wanted. I had my eyes closed, wanting to feel every moment instead of watching it.

As Jabari was kissing near my right earlobe I heard him whisper, "I want to feel inside of you. Are you ready for all this?"

I looked down at his manhood and it was average, but it was rock hard and it was throbbing something fierce. He knew I wanted it, but he wanted to hear me say it, so I did. "Yes Jabari, I am ready. I am so ready." I swear we made love on that couch for hours. I didn't know why, but I always fell in love after good sex. It was something about some good loving that always had me wide-open, and Jabari knew how to lay it down.

CHAPTER 19
ARNOLD

I almost died when I turned on the television and I saw my picture pop up, on TMZ with allegations of me being gay. I couldn't believe Carl would sell me out like that. He'd gone to the highest bidder with pictures of me and Pablo hanging out with each other. What was also surprising was TMZ had done their research on Pablo and reported that he was kicked off the Dominican Republic 2016 Olympic team on solicitation allegations of an Olympic Official. To make matters worse they were dubbing Pablo as a high price Dominican male escort that had just moved to the United States. TMZ was reporting that I was procuring Pablo's services on the down-low to hide my sexuality.

That couldn't be further from the truth. Most of the story was false, and I knew this story was very damaging. I had been receiving calls all morning regarding this story. I don't really get on the internet or belong to any of the popular social media sites, but I'd been told that this story had broken the internet. I knew I was going to be the laughing stock of the team, once I entered the players' locker room. I prayed that my teammates would treat me with dignity and respect, but I wasn't holding my breath on that.

I had just received a call from my coach informing me to turn on the television, and that I had a meeting with him and the ownership entity in two hours. I didn't know what to expect from this meeting, but I was hoping for the best. I also wasn't sure if I was going to deny the allegations or just come clean. I immediately called Pablo and got voicemail. I wanted to talk to him about all the escorting allegations, and if they were true. Pablo had never asked me for money, so I was trying to keep an open mind and not jump to conclusions.

I also tried dialing Carl's cell phone. I even called his mother's house and I didn't get an answer. I couldn't believe this fool would set me up like this. After all I had done for him. I allowed him to live rent free for several months, and the countless after countless loans I afforded him that I knew I would never get back. I even worked out with him, helping to get his ankle back on target to possibly play in the NBA or at least overseas again. *Where was the loyalty? Why would he betray me like this? Was he really that jealous of Pablo?*

I guess I was the fool for not believing him last week, when he threatened to go public about me and Pablo if I kicked him out. I really thought he was bluffing; especially after he'd offered to hook up with me in exchange for the living arrangement. I could very well out him as well, but he didn't have very much to lose I guess. Carl had better stay the hell away from me; because when I caught up with him, that ankle wasn't going to be the only thing in pain on his body.

I took a quick shower and prepared for the unexpected at my meeting with my coach and the owners of the Washington Wizards. When I got to the arena, my agent was already sitting there on the phone. When he saw me, he hurried off the phone and directed his attention to me.

"Arnold this doesn't look good for you at all. What have you gotten yourself into? Who are you hanging out with these days? You have been one of the best clients to work for. I would have never imagined something like this happening with you. You know this could really jeopardize everything we worked so hard for?"

Chad my agent, was a young, slick Italian guy that had reached out to me my sophomore year in college. He said all the right things and made all the right moves; I would had been a fool to not sign with him. He had gotten me in the NBA, with one of the top signing bonuses and salaries for any rookie player this year. I knew I could count on Chad, but I also knew he was about his money and reputation too.

I was scared and embarrassed too. All I could say was, "I don't know what is going on. It's like I woke up this morning to a nightmare. Most of the things the media is reporting is false."

Chad looked at me a little funny and said, "Most? I need for all of this stuff to be false if you want to continue playing in the NBA. I've gotten in contact with the best public relations firm in D.C. That's who I just hung up with, and they're willing to represent you and try to get this story buried and fast."

When Chad and I walked into the players' boardroom at the Capital One arena, Coach Proctor and the owners, who were all middle-aged white men, were seated with their heads facing downward. There was no eye contact whatsoever. The team's legal staff was sitting around the table looking very intimidating. The energy in the room was very gloomy. This was a very different vibe from when I'd signed my contract with the team, with all parties in attendance. There was no champagne, finger foods, or friendly faces.

Tom McKnight from the team's legal counsel broke the ice and started the meeting. "We all know why we are here, and anything discussed in this meeting should remain private, and not discussed anywhere else outside these walls. The NBA and the Wizards' franchise doesn't discriminate against anyone's sexual preference. We want to make that crystal clear. What any player does in their personal lives is their business. We don't want to assume anything nor are we asking you to admit to anything, today. What this meeting is for is to figure out how you want to handle this very private matter that is being played out in public, especially the media?

"There will be a lot of attention on tonight's game because of the accusations that were disclosed today from various media outlets. This is not the sort of attention that our organization would like to attract. Our main focus should be on our athletes' performances on the court, and the teams' winning and losing streak. Unfortunately, your story is overshadowing what's really important. We want to be clear that it's your decision to play tonight, but we would advise against it. Some of your teammates have already reached out to the coach and the ownership that they don't want to play with you.

"We don't agree with their decisions, but we don't want to cause dissention amongst the team, which is why we are prepared to offer you a buyout. We plan to honor your first-year salary. If you walk away from the team and become a free agent, you will receive five million dollars after you sign this agreement that you will not seek any legal action against the team or the NBA." Tom placed the contract in front of me and my agent as he continued to lay out the details. "You also will not be able to make any statements to the media pertaining to this agreement or any derogatory statements that pertain to the NBA or this franchise."

It took everything inside of me to not breakdown in tears after hearing the end of my basketball career flash before my eyes. I was in a state of shock and couldn't utter any words from my mouth. Chad saw in my face that something was wrong with me and spoke up for me. "This is absolutely not going down like this. My client plans on playing tonight. He has been averaging ten to eleven points per game, which is above average for all rookies this season. The Wizard's franchise and the team would be at a disadvantage if they lost Arnold."

Chad and I walked out of that meeting feeling a little defeated. I didn't want to stop playing, but I also didn't want all this scrutiny on who I was or wasn't dating either. Chad left me and told me not to worry. Chad's parting advice, was just to act like nothing happened, and eventually all this would die down. I was really hoping that it did and sooner rather than later.

When it came time for tonight's game, I came to the arena already dressed. Paparazzi was greater than normal when I arrived. I had to dodge paparazzi heading into the arena. I knew they were there trying to get a statement to appease their readers, watchers, or listeners on the latest pro athlete scandal. I wasn't about to give them any information to miss quote. I trusted Chad and I would let this new PR firm deal with the media. I was going to focus on playing basketball, which was my first and only love.

In the player parking garage, and right before I got out my car to head inside the arena I called Pablo one more time to see what he had to say for himself. To no avail, his phone went directly to voicemail. This was really bothering me, because Pablo would normally pick up on the first ring when I called. He had to be avoiding me and this was very unsettling and making me feel that there could possibly be some truth to what TMZ was reporting about his past.

I knew Pablo was into athletics as well, his body was just too tight and athletic for it to be natural. We even talked about him going to the Olympics briefly. When I would bring up the topic of him playing college or even amateur sports, he would always brush it off or change the subject. When I think about it, Pablo had always been very evasive when I brought up anything about his past, and what really brought him to D.C. from the Dominican Republic.

I didn't even think twice about not going into the locker room with the other players. That was a battle I was going to have to deal with on my own time. I had several uniforms at home and I would just get dressed there or in hotel rooms, until my teammates felt comfortable around me. I wasn't going to lie, I did check some of the players out once or twice, but very discreetly and not in a stalking manner. It was more out of admiration than anything else; but I was sure if I ever admitted to that, it would be taken the wrong way; and I left well enough alone.

We ended up losing to the Atlanta Hawks eighty-eight to ninety-four. When the game began and my team walked onto the court, you could hear all the gay slurs coming from the audience. I heard so many negative comments from "faggot" to "you like to take it in the dookie shoot," that it took a lot for me to just sit there and play. I tried my best to ignore all the comments, but I had to admit that it stung real hard and deep in my core. I had never been publicly humiliated before in my life. Coach decided not to play me until the last few minutes of the game when we were down by twenty points. I managed to get the score back up to only a single digit loss. However, I knew if I had played more throughout the game, we would have won. I guess coach cared more about the team's reputation than actually wining since they decided to bench me almost the entire game.

CHAPTER 20

Halloween had finally arrived; and this year, Halloween happened to land on a Friday. The library was noticeably empty since everyone was probably preparing to enjoy the weekend festivities. The staff at the library was patiently waiting for closing time to pass, so they could rush out those double doors and enjoy their Halloween weekend. Pablo was at work not in the best of moods. Ever since he'd been abruptly pushed into the spotlight, due to Carl's jealous rage, he'd been contacted by the U.S. Immigration and Customs Enforcement, better known as ICE, about possible deportation.

The governmental agency didn't currently have enough hard evidence to deport Pablo immediately based on the prostitution allegations, but they were keeping a close eye on his finances. He was due for another hearing in a couple weeks, in which ICE would make their final assessment. If it weren't for his great relationship with his boss, Chaka, he probably would have already been back on his island. Chaka had provided a positive and insightful testimony as a character witness on Pablo's behalf during his first hearing.

Pablo was cursing the existence of Coach Diego. Pablo, thought, *if only I left that life behind me, I wouldn't be going through this now.* He'd also been avoiding Arnold, because he didn't know how to face him. He was so very sorry about what was going on with him, but he had his own issues to worry about now. Not to mention Angel kept at him, every time he would come into the library Angel would summons him down to the restroom. Angel had gotten so strong Pablo couldn't fight the compulsion.

Pablo thought about just giving up on his American dream and going back to his island on his own accord. He also thought about possibly moving to Europe and allowing Jean to take care of him. Ever since they had reconnected, Jean had been contacting him incessantly. They picked up right where they'd left off. Pablo decided to let bygones be bygones and accepted Jean back into his life permanently. Jean appeared to be pretty regretful, and of course the money and gifts that he showered down on Pablo made it almost impossible not to forgive Jean.

When Pablo had first been contacted by Immigration about possible deportation, he reached out to Jean. Jean told him not to worry and told him that Great Britain was a wonderful place to live. He said the least he could do was sponsor him in his own country; so, he didn't have to move back to the Dominican Republic, where things were a lot harder to make a living. Especially since Pablo had been black balled in the Dominican Republic after the Olympic scandal. Pablo was really hoping that he could stay in the

United States, he actually liked it here. It was just that too many bad things were happening that was out of his control.

Pablo felt like any day now, his body could possibly not be his own anymore. Every time he found himself in the bathroom facing Angel in the mirror he thought, the day had arisen. Angel had been getting stronger and stronger and Pablo didn't think that Angel would wait for Halloween. Now that Halloween had finally come, Pablo was terrified. He was hoping that he could get out of the library today without having to see Angel. When Pablo had woken up this morning he wanted to call out sick, but he knew that he needed to continue to make a good impression for his boss Chaka. She'd done so much for him, and he didn't want to let her down. Pablo had no clue if it would be him or Arnold that Angel wanted. He also didn't know that Angel was in the basement this very moment waiting for the perfect time to perform his final sacrifice. This was something Angel had been working very hard for, for the last sixteen years.

Chaka kept guaranteeing Pablo that he didn't have anything to worry about. She had just reassured him yesterday that she was close to vanquishing Angel. Chaka had started the process of cleansing her body and soul from all things unholy. This had definitely taken a toll on her relationship with Grant. She started seeing Grant less and less since she decided to stop having sex with him.

She knew that there was a possibility that Grant wouldn't stick around for a sexless relationship. Chaka however, hoped that he would have come to the realization that he couldn't live without her and their love-making, and he would propose. However, several weeks had passed and she was hearing from him less and less; and only saw him one other time after their last lunch date. Life for Chaka hadn't slowed down though, she had been doing nonstop research on paranormal activity. Father Kind and Chaka had met a few times and she'd even taken him back to the lower level men's restroom in hopes to catch Angel in action.

Angel still hadn't revealed himself while Father Kind was present, and this was what was keeping them from getting rid of him. Father Kind needed to see what he was dealing with. There were so many different types of demons and evil spirits out there. They had tried so many different rituals and scriptures, but nothing had worked. Chaka was not the type of person to give up, and she had been devoting most of her energy toward getting rid of Angel; and for good.

Chaka had given both Curtis and Pablo assignments she needed their help on to complete for the week. She had noticed that they weren't as buddy-buddy as they had been in the past. However, Chaka was so distracted with everything else she didn't plan on figuring out what was going on between those two. As long as they were doing their jobs and the drama didn't affect their job functions, she told her self she wouldn't pry.

Chaka wanted to ask Curtis if he had any dealings with Angel, but since he seemed to be unaffected by what was going on, Chaka decided to leave it alone. Chaka didn't know how many of the library staff had been affected by Angel's presence in the library. Nobody had ever come to her about Angel, but that didn't matter to her. She was almost certain that Angel would terrorize anyone that he could. Chaka, however, didn't make a big announcement to the library staff, because she didn't want to get everyone all anxious, nor did she want folks to think she was crazy. So, she kept what was going on to herself for now.

Father Kind had told Chaka that since today was Halloween, that it was probably a bad day to try and vanquish Angel. He informed her that Angel most likely was the strongest he would ever be, on this day, and it would be an insurmountable challenge. Still Chaka didn't care. She wanted Angel out, and she felt confident that she had the right scripture. She also felt like she had cleansed herself from all sin and evil, so that she could perform God's divine will, and that was getting rid of Angel.

Chaka walked into the men's restroom with no fear, and no thought of anyone else possibly being in there. She assumed since it was slow in the library she was sure nobody was down in the basement. However, when she got inside she saw Angel out from inside the mirror. Chaka didn't know if she wanted to run out of the bathroom or stay and fight.

Chaka, got her bearings, took a deep breath and decided she was going to get rid of this demon once and for all. Angel seeing Chaka enter the restroom once again he became infuriated. "Why do I have to keep saying the same thing over and over again? I see you're a very hard-headed fat bitch. I am going to have to teach you a lesson, you picked the wrong day to come up in here."

Chaka tried her best to stick to her plan and ignore Angel, and not let him scare her. She started her prayer, "In Jesus Christ I break and loose Angel and this library from all curses and evil spirits caused by charms, hexes, spells, sorcery, witchcraft, violence, trauma, and rejection. I know that I can never be Mary or Ruth; but God, I ask that you bless me with the power to defeat all my enemies and evil spirits that don't edify your kingdom."

Angel started laughing, "Look you wildebeest, get your hungry ass out of here." Angel knew he couldn't harm Chaka. She had a covering over her, that he couldn't penetrate, and this only made Angel more upset. He did, however, have the power to change the air and the temperature in the room to try and force Chaka out. He made it very windy and hot. Making it hard for Chaka to stable herself in the restroom. She tried to hold on to anything that was fastened to the floor so she wouldn't hurt herself. Chaka held on to the faucet for dear life as the wind beneath her wouldn't allow her to stand up straight. She continued Chanting, "I renounce, break, loose, and rebuke this library from all demonic forces."

The wind was too forceful for her to continue hanging on and she was ushered out of the restroom. Once she was on the outside the door slammed behind her. Chaka wanted to go back inside, but she knew she may be fighting a non-winning battle. She decided to go back upstairs and regain her energy and composure, but she was planning to come back down there before the library closed. Chaka made up her mind that today was the day that this had to end.

When Chaka got upstairs she was limping. She had hurt her leg, as she was being forced out of the men's restroom. Curtis had saw her limping as she was coming out of the elevator. He'd seen her earlier and she was fine so he asked, "What happen to you? Why are you limping? Can I get you anything?"

Chaka replied while struggling through her pain, "I'll be okay, nothing for you to worry about. How are the mailings going for the library's annual pledge fundraiser? Do you think you and Pablo will have them all out before you leave today?"

"We are trying our best to get them done for you today. I haven't seen Pablo in a while. He went to lunch, and I haven't seen him comeback yet."

Chaka then said, "Try and find Pablo for me please. I need to talk with him and please tell him that it's urgent. I need to see him in my office in five minutes."

Curtis was annoyed that he had to go hunting for Pablo. Pablo was the last person he wanted to talk to. Curtis had been doing everything in his power to be cordial to Pablo. He saw on the internet what Pablo had been going through, and it all kind of made sense now where all the so called complimentary hotel rooms had come from. Curtis definitely didn't want to kick anyone while they were down, but he wasn't ready to forgive and make amends with Pablo either.

When Curtis made it to the lobby area of the library, it was completely empty. He went out the glass doors to see if Pablo was out on a smoke break, which he would do periodically. When he didn't see Pablo standing outside he came back inside, and a few moments later, Arnold was walking into the library. Curtis walked up to Arnold and said, "Where is Pablo? Chaka our boss is looking for him at the moment."

Arnold responded, "I was just getting ready to ask you the same thing. I haven't spoken to Pablo since the news broke of our relationship. I am sure you two must have discussed it."

"No, we haven't discussed the unfortunate drama, but I did hear about it on the internet. I am so sorry you have to go through this in the media. I know things must be really difficult for you."

"Curtis man, you don't even know the half of it. I had to temporarily leave the NBA. Something I worked my whole life for. It really is like a nightmare, and on top of everything; the one person that I thought would have my back through this is avoiding me. Do you know why Pablo is avoiding me?"

Curtis didn't really want to get in the middle of what was going on between Pablo and Arnold. However, he was still upset about the betrayal that he experienced from both Pablo and London. So, Curtis thought why not spill the beans to Arnold about his precious Pablo. "I am sorry to be the bearer of bad news, but I don't think Pablo is the person you think he is. All this time I was looking up to him, thinking he was like an older brother, and looking out for me, he was sleeping with my boyfriend behind my back. He was sleeping with him during the same time he was dating you. Looks like we were both made out to look like a fool."

Arnold didn't know what to say. He didn't want to believe what Curtis had just told him, but something was telling him that Curtis was telling the truth. There were so many undesirable things about Pablo that were coming to surface. Arnold had thought maybe he'd opened up to soon and didn't practice enough discretion when it came to Pablo. Arnold thought by coming to Pablo's job he could force Pablo to talk to him, and finally get some answers.

Arnold had left his team and decided to take the contract buyout. He tried to go through the motions and act like nothing happened. However, the pressure from the team's homophobic fans and other players in the NBA were just too overwhelming. He didn't know what his next move would be or what he wanted to do with his millions. His life was basketball and he never thought about doing anything other than that. His agent said that he received offers to play overseas where his sexuality wouldn't be scrutinized as much as it was in the U.S.

Arnold wasn't sure about anything as of yet, he was depressed and needed time to figure out his next move. He had a meeting scheduled with some other players who had been ostracized in the NBA because of their sexuality as well. It was a small group of guys that for whatever reason had experienced something similar. They reached out to him about a possible business opportunity. They said it was very hush-hush at the moment and could only be discussed in person. Arnold had agreed to the meeting, because he wanted to hear what they were offering if anything.

Curtis continued to speak, "Well I've been looking all over the place for Pablo and I have yet to locate him. The only place I haven't checked was the lower level, we can check down there together." Curtis was hoping Pablo wasn't down there, but he wanted to check just in case. He didn't want to disappoint Chaka and go back to her office without

Pablo. Curtis thought, *whatever Chaka needed Pablo for must be very important.*

Arnold agreed to go to the lower level in search for Pablo against his better judgment. He didn't want to have to deal with possibly running into Angel, who hadn't stopped haunting him at night. Arnold was doing the best he could to maintain his sanity with everything that was hitting him at once. Angel was just another thorn in his ass that he wanted desperately to get rid of but didn't know what he could do to stop Angel.

Arnold thought about asking Curtis if he had any dealing with Angel, but he left well enough alone. He just wanted to find Pablo and possibly put some closure to this disastrous story that was trying to destroy his life and reputation. Arnold had already figured out by now, by Pablo's avoidance that most things being reported were probably true. However, he couldn't help that he still felt some sort of love toward Pablo, and just wanted to look him in his eyes and hear the truth no matter how fucked up it was.

Curtis and Arnold checked all the conference rooms in the lower level before they finally checked the men's restroom. When they opened the door, they saw Angel outside of the mirror for the first time with his hands pressed up against Pablo's chest. They both stood there in shock unable to move. They weren't sure what was actually going on, but they had enough sense to know that it wasn't good.

Curtis spoke first, "What's going on in here? Chaka is looking for Pablo, I think he should go upstairs and see what she wants it seems very important."

Angel turned his focus from Pablo to Curtis and said, "Chaka will be fine, Pablo is busy. Today is the day I reclaim my life back on earth and leave this mirror and bathroom behind for good. I've decided that Pablo is the body that I will inhabit. That means Arnold you are off the hook, and you're free to go on with your life as you so choose. I see

Pablo has already done a good job of pissing off the both of you, with his lies and deceit. Curtis, he slept with your man, all the while pretending to be the perfect BFF. Arnold, Pablo has destroyed your thriving basketball career, all the while pretending to be in love with you and hiding the fact that he is a high-paid whore in the process."

Pablo was standing there scared. He had been immobilized by Angel's powers that were trying to find the magic to overtake his body. Pablo started crying and begging, "Curtis! Arnold! I am so sorry for my lies, but I don't deserve this hell. Please don't let him do this to me. Please, I didn't mean to lie to either one of you."

Angel started laughing securing his hold on Pablo. "There is nothing they can do to stop this. It is happening, and nobody can stop this. I am way too powerful now. I warned you that it could possibly be you. But your actions Pablo have made this way easier for me. Now stop crying and stand still until this is over."

Arnold finally got enough courage to speak, "After all we shared Pablo, how could you do this to me. This could ruin me; did you stop to think about your actions? You could have told me. I would have helped you out if you needed money that bad."

Angel continued to laugh and taunt them. "Don't you get it you imbecile? Pablo is selfish, he doesn't care about you. This spineless narcissist only cares about himself and pleasing himself. You were just a pawn in his little game of chest. I've hijacked his game, and it's now check mate for Pablo. You should be thanking me for getting rid of this little liar for you."

Pablo kept pleading, "Arnold please help me. Our relationship wasn't a lie. I love you too. Things in my life were just way too complicated. I didn't think you would accept me if you found out about my past. Trust me, I tried to stop escorting, but I am in the United States all by myself.

The extra money only helped me to live a normal life. Those guys didn't mean anything to me, like you do. It was just a means to an end."

Angel couldn't help himself, "Was it a means to an end when you slept with London, Curtis's man? Tell Arnold how London made love to you harder, stronger, and with way more passion than Arnold could ever! Are you sure it was real or were you just pretending so that you could later embezzle money from him?"

Pablo couldn't contain himself, he was begging Arnold to believe him, "That is not true Arnold, and you know it. I would never do you like that. That's why I kept escorting because I didn't want you to think I was using you. I love you Arnold. London was a mistake. I am so sorry Curtis, I really did think of you as a younger brother I just made a mistake."

Curtis couldn't keep silent any longer, "Look, I don't know what to believe. Part of me thinks, what is happening to you, you deserve for such a horrible person you have been to people. Angel why are you prolonging this, put him out of his misery and take his body. I am tired of hearing him apologize for the things he shouldn't have done in the first place."

Angel smiled and said, "Finally somebody who agrees with me. You're totally right, Curtis he deserves this, more so than me. See I was the victim, falling in love with the bully that tormented me every day in high school. I was dumb back then, but I have a second chance, and I intend to live my life to the fullest now."

Angel repeated something ten times that neither Arnold nor Curtis could understand. Then the bathroom went completely dark. A few seconds later Pablo stepped forward and the motions lights to the restroom came on for a second, then it went dark again. Angel's physical form was replaced by a pale, dark haired woman wearing all black. She looked to be in her sixties. She spoke and broke the silence.

"Angel you have finally given the proper amount of sacrifices to the lord of darkness. Now your wish has been granted. No longer are you a spirit trapped between two worlds. You are of human flesh, willing and able to do whatever you so choose with the time you have left on this earth. In your place your final sacrifice is Pablo."

Then within seconds Pablo's sad face could be seen inside the mirror. Suddenly, the lights of the bathroom came on, and Curtis and Arnold were left standing there alone. They were unsure where Pablo or rather Angel had gone, or the woman in black who had just performed the spell that put Pablo inside the mirror.

CHAPTER 21
ANGEL

The transformation was spectacular and everything I imagined it would be. I was now able to feel the sun as it beamed down on my skin. No longer was I captive in a place where I didn't belong. I had gone through a lot to get here. I didn't think I would ever escape my prison inside that mirror. I also loved my new body. I was cute in my original form, but Pablo's body was everything I'd wish I was growing up. I was light skin, had a killer body, perfect skin, and more importantly I was able to do whatever the hell I wanted to do.

I was never satisfied with my looks but now I was more than satisfied. The first day I walked out of that library, I had my head to the sky. Nothing was going to bring me down, I had a second chance at life. I saw all the stares I got from women and men alike. I could see why Pablo made all the

Marcel Emerson 173

money he did. Shit I would have paid to be with Pablo if I could afford it.

The world around me had changed drastically since I'd been trapped in the mirror. I no longer recognized the city. Everything was so new. There was new construction everywhere. All the new buildings that had been constructed, had me lost. It took me a good little while to figure it all out. Old roads had changed and split into two, freeway entrances had moved. The projects that I had grown up in had been torn down and replaced by brand new townhouses and apartment buildings. There was a Giant Supermarket, iHop, and white people in the hood now.

The trains thank goodness where still the same, although there were more stops added to the redline than I remembered. I guess I shouldn't had been that surprised, they say all things get better over time. Why would I have thought the nation's capital wouldn't do the same? I was so glad that Pablo's address was on his Identification Card in his wallet, and his house keys where in his pants pocket. It made it easy for me to find my new place of residence.

It was nice to live alone and not have to share a bathroom or a room with someone who didn't like me or respect me. Growing up my two older brothers hated that I was so feminine. When I would decorate my side of the room, with the things I liked like Brandy, Monica, Donatella Versace, or anything that had to do with pop divas or fashion they would torment me and tell me that I was making the room too feminine.

Pablo had really nice décor in his place. Everything in his apartment was very modern and contemporary. I loved his style as much as I loved his body. Which was one of the reasons I didn't choose to sacrifice Arnold. Arnold would have posed a serious problem for me, and I wouldn't be able to maintain his lifestyle. I was never good with sports. Pablo was an easy decision, becoming a highly paid escort was something I knew I could do with my eyes closed. I was doing sexual favors for free when I was still in high school. I never even thought about getting paid for it, back then I just wanted the attention and to feel special.

I had been getting several calls from Jean, one of Pablo's clients. The last message sounded frantic. He was upset that Pablo hadn't returned his call in the midst of his pending deportation. I didn't understand fully the gravity of Pablo's immigration troubles before I decided to become him. I thought he had everything worked out. I was unaware that he was in the process of possibly having to move back to Santo Domingo. Frantically, I returned Jean's phone calls and invited him to come over to my new place, Pablo's apartment. I didn't want to be caught in a pricey hotel, considering Pablo was under investigation for prostitution.

Jean was on his way, he had just called and said the car service was almost at the apartment. I was happy to entertain another one of Pablo's clients. The sexual gratification, let alone the cash that I'd been receiving entertaining all of Pablo's clients had been the highlight of my new existence. Not having sex for all those years and missing a man's touch on my body, had turned me back into the sex addict I was as a teenager. I had even had sex with the infamous London. I now see why Pablo didn't want to stop from seeing him, once he found out he was dating Curtis. London by far was the best sexual partner that I had experienced. I didn't know if it was the size of his member or the stroke, but all I knew was that he sent my new body into spasms.

The only thing I didn't like about London was that he was a little too masculine, and hood for me. After having almost been murdered by Jeffrey I wanted to steer clear away from the too macho, almost straight men. I had always had a thing for white men, but never really had the opportunity to date them. However, Pablo's client list consisted of nothing but rich white men, and I was loving this new experience so far.

When Jean walked through the door of my new place, I was pleasantly surprised. He was a very handsome white man, with a very nice physique. Jean had long sandy brown hair, and the warmest boyish smile. I loved his British accent too. I couldn't wait to see what was underneath his clothes. Jean was all worried about Pablo's pending case with immigration, that he was kind of ruining the mood for me. That's all he wanted to discuss. I probably should had been more concerned with the possibility of having to leave the U.S., but I was just so engrossed with my new life I didn't think about it as much, until Jean kept pressing the issue. He kept asking me why I didn't seem more worried than I was.

Jean continued to press the issue, "So Pablo, you are telling me since the last we spoke you haven't heard anything about your current immigration status?"

I lied, because I didn't want Jean to know that I wasn't taking this seriously, "Nope, they haven't contacted me about it. They probably have a lot more things to worry about than lil 'ole me." This was far from the truth. I had been bombarded with calls from immigration as to why I haven't been to work. The case manager assigned to Pablo's case had called me every day since I'd been in his body.

I didn't have anything to say to them, so I avoided the calls. I could only assume that Chaka had reported that I hadn't been to work. She probably was going through the roof since her precious employee Pablo was now trapped inside that mirror in my place. There was no way I was stepping foot back into that library. I knew Pablo worked there, but I was making way more than enough money escorting.

Jean continued some more, "Well I guess since they aren't harassing you anymore, you don't need my help in relocating you to Europe. I was sure you would love living in London. It's a marvelous place, full of life and culture. The city is a lot older than any city hear in America. It's also full of so many things I am sure you would enjoy. So, if things ever get too difficult for you, do not hesitate to contact me. I would be more than willing to help you out in any way that I can."

This was good to know—Jean was the real deal. He had the means to move me overseas without any hesitation. I kind of liked my new-found independence, so I wasn't too quick to become someone's concubine. I enjoyed the fact that once the night was over, I was on my own to do whatever I so choose. I was gracious, though, you never knew if I would need Jean later on down the road. "You are far too kind, Jean. What would I do without you?"

Jean kind of looked at me and did a double take. He then said, "Pablo something seems very different about you, today. You don't even speak with the slightest bit of a Spanish accent anymore."

This was the first time I had come encounter with someone who had known Pablo that noticed the difference. I tried my best to play it off, "Jean I am such a quick study. Everyone finds English to be a hard language to learn. However, I love a challenge and I find this language very easy to speak—especially now that I live here in the United States."

Jean kept looking at me weird and kept pressing the issue, "It's not even the lack of accent. You have an entirely different demeanor than before. If I wasn't looking at you, I wouldn't even think I was talking to the same Pablo I've known all these years."

was tired of this back and forth, and I was bored. Jean was right, but there was no way he knew what really happened and I wasn't about to explain it to him. I changed the subject to something that I knew he would enjoy. "Enough about who I used to be and let me show you the new and improved me. Take off all your clothes and from here on out refer to me as Angel. That is what I want to be called now, it's my new American name."

Jean was more than eager to follow my instructions. Within seconds he had all his clothes off, and he was standing in front of me with a hard on that could poke someone's eyes out. I got on my knees and glided over to where he was standing on my hardwood floors. When I got close enough I engulfed his member with my mouth, using the no hands method, and started moving my head up and down the shaft in slow, but steady motion. I could tell this was driving Jean crazy because he couldn't help from moaning.

I looked up for a moment, and I saw his eyes closed and he had a very satisfied smile on his face as I continued pleasing him. An hour later we lay across my bed holding each other, sweat glistening from our bodies from all the physical contact and gyrating that had just transpired.

Right before I passed out Jean said, "Angel we have never had sex like this before. I am not sure what has gotten into you, but I think I am falling in love with the new you. You sure I can't convince you to move oversees with me?"

CHAPTER 22
CHAKA

I was on cloud nine and I couldn't be happier. I had to say to myself, Chaka, *patience is a virtue and obedience garners results* are my new mantras to live by. I couldn't believe how on time God's grace could be. Glory be to God! He answers prayers and He will provide for, all your needs. I held steadfast to my beliefs and do you know I am on my way to Atlantic City to elope with the man of my dreams. Grant asked me to marry him, and I said yes. Not six months or a year from now, he wanted to make me his wife as soon as possible. Yes, I had to pinch myself too, just to make sure I wasn't dreaming.

It had been almost two months of Grant and I barely talking and hardly getting together like I was getting used to. I thought maybe our relationship had run its course, and he was on to the next promiscuous woman. Boy was I wrong, and was glad about it too; even though I hated being wrong. I was going to be someone's wife, something that I never thought would happen to me.

Grant picked me up and we made the three hour drive to Atlantic City from my townhouse. I was on the edge of my seat the entire trip. Even though we were driving up all set to seal the deal. I was still in disbelief that we were driving to get married. Grant picked me up last night and took me to my favorite restaurant and popped the question. He opened all the way up to me and revealed that his life would be empty without me in it. He said he couldn't live without me, something I'd never heard anyone ever say to me, Chaka, before.

We checked into Caesar's Palace and I was delighted to be in one of their honey-moon suites. As much as I would have liked to be on a tropical island celebrating this moment, I was just happy that this moment was occurring. Grant was kind of rushing to get this underway because when we left Atlantic City the following day, Grant had to go on tour with his band. He would be away for a week traveling to Houston for a Jazz Festival and then to New Orleans to perform at a music conference.

I suggested we wait until he came back, but he said this was something he wanted to do and should have done by now. Who was I to protest a man in love with a woman? The bible says, "He who finds a wife, finds a good thing, and obtains favor from the Lord." I couldn't agree more with this proverb, nor did I want to impede on Grants favor from God. Caesar's Place had a small chapel in their large Atlantic City property that fit us nicely.

The minister performing our ceremony was an older Italian man with salt and pepper hair. He smiled at us with gentle eyes as we walked in to recite our vows. Both Grant and I were in tears as we became husband in wife, with only the minister and a Caesar's Palace employee there serving as our one and only witness. We stayed in our room the entire night consummating our marriage. It was so nice to make love to Grant as his wife instead of his girlfriend. When we finished our love making this time, I no longer felt guilty about giving myself to him. I now belonged to him and he belonged to me.

The day after my wedding day, I was still on cloud nine; even though I had just dropped Grant off at the airport. I knew he would be back soon and that we had so much more time on this earth together to look forward to. I still had my busy life to attend to and considering I was the newly elected president of my homeowners' association; there was one particular fire I needed to put out.

The previous president had stolen money from the association, and we didn't have enough money to pay the bills. I had given him till today to come up with the money that he had laundered, or I threatened to contact the police. Of course, he did what he needed to do, robbed Peter to pay Paul. I didn't really care where the money came from as long as he returned it back to the association, so I could get these bills paid. If it wasn't one thing it was another. A tremendous weight was lifted off of me when the previous president presented me with a check for the stolen money. I was able to feel good regarding one fire I had managed to extinguish, because the Lord knows I didn't have the time nor patience to have to escalate this matter.

I hadn't forgotten about the drama that was going on at work either. I didn't know how I was going to solve the problem that I was currently dealing with there. Unfortunately, Angel was able to perform the dark magic he needed to escape his prison inside the mirror. In his place he had put my dear employee Pablo, who was inside the mirror now at the library. I couldn't believe right underneath my nose Angel had possessed and took over Pablo's human body and was out on these streets probably running wild.

He chose not to come to work as Pablo, which was probably for the best, because I probably would have killed him on site, and gone to jail. I did, however, notify the authorities that Pablo hadn't reported to work in weeks. Since he was on a work visa to live in the United States, he was facing immediate deportation. I had gone to visit the real Pablo inside the mirror several times since he'd been held captive.

Pablo informed me that the same witch that put Angel behind the mirror in the first place came to visit him, shortly after the switch. She told him that he could escape his prison, by performing the same human sacrifices that Angel had done and found a replacement for himself. Pablo was so distraught at his fate that I wasn't sure what he was going to do. I had spoken to Father Kind about what had occurred, and Father Kind told me that what was done was done, there was no way of getting Pablo back into his body.

Father Kind said that Pablo was just as good as dead, and that I would need to muster up the strength to vanquish him, or he would start doing the same things Angel had done all these years. I kept replaying Father Kind's warning in my head, *"Be very cautious of what comes out of Pablo's mouth now. He is no longer the Pablo you once knew. His soul has now been taken over by the devil. He's now a demon living between two worlds. I know you feel sorry for him, and you should. I wouldn't wish this on my worst enemy. However, Pablo had just enough evil inside of him for the devil to take control. Had he cleansed himself and gave his life over to the Lord, this would have never occurred. I am not saying its Pablo's fault, but it is his fate. Remember, you cannot play with evil. Once the devil comes knocking don't ever answer."*

Father Kind kept telling me that I had the power to vanquish any demon that crossed my path. He was certain that I was cut from the same cloth as my father and that I just had to believe in my abilities and surrender fully unto the Lord. I was so unsure of my abilities, and I wasn't sure if Father Kind knew what he was talking about. However, I had been attending Alfred Street Baptist Church in Alexandria, Virginia, ever since I allowed Pablo to be taken over by Angel. I felt so guilty and powerless the only thing I could do was turn to God.

It was very rewarding to receive a good word on a regular basis. I had forgotten how a Sunday service could really recharge your mind, body, and spirit. I had initially stopped going to church regularly because I thought I could just have a personal relationship with God, by praying and doing my best to keep his commandments. However, there was something about organized weekly spiritual edification that just kept you renewed, and on track with God.

I am not going to lie, I didn't always keep God's word, and it was very easy for me to fall astray. However, I now had a renewed relationship with God and it felt wonderful. I used to think that my weight and my physical appearance, and being a dark-skinned woman was keeping me from marriage. Not to mention, I was relying on God's grace and mercy to get me through life, because I wasn't living right. But, God had spoken to me the night after I let Grant know that we would no longer be fornicating as an unmarried couple. God came to me in a dream and said, "Chaka, if you love me you will keep my word. You have everything you need in life."

God's words didn't take me long to understand and apply to my life. I knew I wasn't perfect, but I also knew better, but I wasn't doing better. After I received Grant's proposal, I finally understood what God meant by, "I will give you peace that passes all understanding."

I knew what I had to do. As much as I wanted to save Pablo from his fate. That was just not what God had in store for Pablo's life. I didn't know everything about Pablo, but he was a great worker, and I didn't wish his fate on my worst enemy, but what was done was done. I needed to cast Pablo's spirit and that black magic that put him inside that mirror out of the library and for good. You could only serve one God and that was Jesus Christ.

CHAPTER 23
CURTIS

Things were going good for me. I was acing all my classes. I was finally enjoying a friendship with someone who I felt loved me for who I was and didn't want to take advantage of my kindness or my inexperience. Jabari was so easy to get along with. Once things started to get serious between Jabari and me, I introduced him to my mom and Dr. Wilson. Thankfully, to my joy and amazement, both of them loved Jabari.

I was a little afraid at first because I thought they were going to think I was too young to be dating someone in their thirties, but Jabari charmed the pants off of both of them. He is very responsible and respectful at the same time. After witnessing what happened to Pablo, as well as my part in getting Jeffrey killed, and his kids now being raised without a father, I took some time to reflect on my life. These past several months had me self-reflecting hard on what I was and wasn't proud of. Although Angel scared the hell out of me, and he wouldn't stop antagonizing me by haunting my dreams and thoughts, I should have never involved myself in his ploy.

I was far from a devil worshiper and I knew better than to get involved in something so evil. London was not worth damning my soul to hell for eternity. London had the nerve to contact me after three months of working at the hotel near the library. Apparently, he had been fired and needed my help. When I asked him what had happened, he confessed and said that he'd gotten caught in one of the rooms with a hotel guest. The cleaning staff was prohibited from being in guests' rooms with the doors closed. This wasn't London's first time working in a hotel. He knew there were cameras everywhere.

I wasn't shocked about the turn of events, karma was that bitch that would always get you when you knew you was dead ass wrong. The funny thing was London had the nerve to ask me for help so he could remain in D.C., until he get got back on his feet. There was no way I was helping someone who had done me so wrong, and I told him just that. He had called me a few times after, but I wasn't accepting anymore phone calls from London. Now I wasn't sure if he moved or if he was still in the area. Honestly, I didn't care either, I was done with folks trying to take advantage of me.

When I was leaving work today I ran into Angel. I was shocked to see him, since he decided to go AWOL from work. I don't know why I thought he would pick up as Pablo and continue working at the library. But I guess Angel had better things to do with his time. I never thought I would see him again; or at least I hoped, I would never see him again after he hadn't shown up at work for weeks.

When Angel saw me leave the library he motioned for me to come over to where he was standing. Against my better judgement, I did what he asked me to do. I wasn't sure if he still had powers or was he just as human as Pablo and I were. I rolled my eyes when I got to where he was standing and said, "What the hell do you want Angel? I did everything you asked me to do, and I already feel terrible about it. Haven't you used me enough already, considering you stole another person's body?"

Angel wore a smirk of satisfaction on his face when he responded, "No need to feel bad, Pablo got what he deserved. You know what he did to you, and he was nothing more than a male prostitute. But anyway, I didn't come here to discuss Pablo. I need some help."

I looked at Angel like he was crazy. "Haven't I helped you enough? I don't want no part in whatever scheme or evil you now have up your sleeve. I've already done things that I am not proud of, so no I won't help you."

"This is funny, so now you're Mother Theresa all of a sudden? Don't start acting all holier than thou with me. You and I can be the friends that you and Pablo were supposed to be. I would never sleep with any of my friends' significant others, and I am sure we can have way more fun than you and Pablo ever had."

I was beginning to get irritated, "What part of no don't you comprehend, the N or the O? I am trying to be more of a positive person these days, and from the looks of things you aren't on my level."

"Look Curtis, I need you. Please, I don't have anyone else to turn to. Because of your stupid ass boss Chaka, Pablo is being pursued by Immigration. They want Pablo's ass back in the Dominican Republic. You know I don't speak a lick of Spanish. Please Curtis you have to help me."

"Chaka? What does Chaka have to do with any of this?"

"That's the same thing I been wondering ever since she walked her fat ass in the men's bathroom and tried to vanquish me when I was still trapped inside the mirror. She is some sort of "good" witch or something. Shit, I don't know what the hell she is, but she has immigration on my ass. I had to leave Pablo's apartment because the authorities had come to abduct me. Luckily, I escaped down the fire escape, but I could be in some federal detention somewhere, waiting to go to a country I know nothing about. I don't have anywhere to go or a place to stay. The authorities have seized all of Pablo's assets. I can't get into his bank account or use his credit cards anymore.

"I had to get rid of his cell phone too, because I wasn't sure if they could track that and find my location. I have almost ten thousand dollars in cash. I can pay you, if you can just help me get a place or secure a hotel somewhere under your name until I figure out a plan."

Angel was crazy if he thought I was going to put anything in my name for him. He better figure it out on his own; and fast, if he didn't want to be deported. I for one, was no longer getting myself involved in his foolishness. I also had no idea that Chaka had known all along what was going on. She'd never said anything to me about Angel. However, that wasn't even the issue at hand. The issue was getting away from Angel and fast.

"Look Angel, I cannot be of any help to you. I don't own any credit cards," I lied. "Since I don't have any credit, there is no way I could get you an apartment or any housing in my name. I wish you the best, but I really have to go," I lied.

Angel's attitude changed from desperate to rage. He looked like he could poke my eyes out, but at this point I was willing to take whatever he could dish out. "Look you weak son of bitch you owe me your life. It could have been your body I jumped into, but I spared your life and look where it got me."

I started walking away, "Look Angel I already said no. Leave me the hell alone and don't ever come back to my place of work ever again, or I will be the one to call immigration my damn self and have them come down here and ship your evil ass away." I got away from Angel and to the Metro as fast as I could. I looked back a few times to see if I was being followed—thankfully I wasn't.

I suspected since Angel was down and out on his luck his powers had gone away as soon as he inhabited Pablo's body. Served him right too, considering all that he had done in order to get in that body. All the lives he had sacrificed, families that he had left in mourning, and corpses that were never discovered. I guess Angel was getting what he deserved, but I was just happy he was out of my thoughts and dreams. I knew I would someday have to answer for my involvement in it, and I was hoping God took mercy on my soul on my day of reckoning.

When Jabari picked me up from the Congress Heights metro station near his house, he could tell something was up with me. He started questioning me, "Baby what's the matter; you look like you seen a ghost or something? Did something happen to you while you were on the train?"

I had confided in Jabari early on in our relationship what had gone down with the whole Angel, Pablo, Jeffery, and London fiasco. I didn't think he would believe me because the story sounded so farfetched, but Jabari said he did. Which was another reason why I loved him so much, we could talk about anything. So, I told him what had just happened, "Angel had ambushed me as I was getting off from work." I continued with the story until we got to his place to relax for the weekend.

What I liked most about Jabari was that he believed me wholeheartedly. He never second guessed anything I said, and he trusted me fully. I wasn't afraid to tell him anything. Even the most embarrassing things Jabari wouldn't laugh or make me feel bad. He was so easy to talk to, which was a good thing; because I never felt like I had that before. Most people when they found out who you really were or found out your deepest darkest secrets, they would try to use them against you or judge and label you.

I didn't know how long this fairy tell was going to last with Jabari. I was hoping it would last forever; because something this good, I had better hold onto it as long as I had the opportunity. I was a little afraid to go to sleep at night after bumping into Angel; but luckily, I woke up well rested with no dream invasions from Angel. I guess Angel was truly helpless and his powers were completely gone.

CHAPTER 24
ARNOLD

They say everything happens for a reason, and my public outing wasn't as bad as I'd initially thought it would be. When one door closes another one will surely open, and that is just what was happening to me. The couple of weeks following the revelation of my sexuality to the world, because of Carl's petty ass, was really hard for me. The fans and some of the players made it almost impossible for me to play during the games.

I was constantly tormented every time I stepped onto the court. I was called everything in the book accept a child of God. I was hurt at first because I was beginning to gain a hometown fan base. But as soon as the news dropped about me potentially being gay, everyone who initially supported me, didn't anymore. It had gotten so bad that at the last game I played, a fan had actually thrown feces on the court, and had to be escorted out of the arena. While the fan was being escorted out of the arena by security, he was shouting the most hateful things toward me, and the crowd instead of booing was cheering him on.

Thankfully my agent was heaven sent and brought me some good news just when I thought about giving up hope. Unbeknownst to me, there had already been talks and negotiations already in place to develop a team for openly gay players in the NBA. Unfortunately, the NBA had been homophobic for some time now and folks like myself had been ostracized and felt left out of opportunities to really shine on the basketball court. I'd found this out during the meeting that I had with some of the ousted NBA players. When my agent brought this to my attention, I almost laughed in his face. An actual entire professional basketball team built up with nothing but gay ball players was unbelievable.

Apparently, my situation wasn't an isolated incident, and many players had been subjected to the same kind of treatment that I was going through. They didn't want to give up their dream of playing professional basketball in America, nor did they want to be bullied from the sport that they loved. These players wanted vindication, and they had gone to significant lengths to ensure that they showed America that they could play just as good as anyone else in the league.

The all-gay basketball team was owned by the gay billionaire Kyle Trophy. Kyle had made his money in television, having produced critically acclaimed shows and documentaries for several networks. Trophy had just signed a deal with Netflix that was worth five hundred million dollars. Trophy's pockets and influence were deep. He managed to get the NBA to license his franchise and team, and he was also able to get Washington, D.C.'s government to approve the new arena. The new arena was going to be housed in an impoverished area of the city, which would bring a lot of opportunity to its residents.

I'd recently met with the coach and owner of the new team, right after I decided that I could no longer take the humiliation I was receiving playing for the Wizards. They were delighted to give me a contract. Unfortunately, since we were a new team they weren't able to match what I was getting from the Wizards. However, they promised me that once the team proved themselves, increased salaries and bonuses would follow after the first year. After I signed on the dotted line, the team roster was presented to me.

I was very impressed by the list of names that had already agreed to launch this new team. Some of these guys I had played against while I was in college and had no clue of their sexuality. I didn't really know what to expect, but I was confident in the roster that I saw that the team would do well in its first year. Every player on the team should have been a first round draft pick any season they entered the NBA draft. However, due to politics and their sexuality, many of these players sat on the sidelines watching instead of playing.

Everything seemed to be working out for me, considering everything that I had gone through. My parents, who I thought would take this the hardest, were actually very supportive. They weren't disappointed one bit, they supported me as much as they could and wished me all the success in the world with my new team. I had recently just purchased my first home. It was a single-family home in a new development in an area called Congress Heights, in Southeast, Washington, D.C. My agent suggested it would be a good look for me to purchase a home in the community where the new basketball arena would be opening up.

The community I chose were newly constructed homes, and I would be the first person to live in my home, and I liked the thought of that. I would be able to create my own positive energy in my home, and it would be devoid of past spirits. Considering what I had gone through with Angel, I wanted to stay clear of evil spirits or paranormal activity. I was moving out of my apartment today to move into my new home. I lucked out and was able to move into a home that was under contract from a buyer that fell through on the payments.

I was really excited to be moving out of my apartment. This apartment; although it was very nice, and in a nice area of the city, brought back too many unpleasant memories. When I was in my apartment, all I could think about was Carl and Pablo, and how both of them disappointed me. Not to mention, it was very close to where the Wizards played. I knew I needed to talk to someone about what I had just gone through, but I felt like I really needed to change my environment first and then maybe speak to a therapist.

I had packed up the last of my personal belongings, and the movers were almost finished with moving the heavy furniture out of the apartment and onto their truck. When everything was completely moved out, I did one last walkthrough of the place. As I was about to walk out the door, I was startled when I saw Carl walk inside the apartment. He must have gotten into the building by the movers, since this was a very secure building. I hadn't talked to Carl since I kicked his ass out, so I wasn't sure what he wanted.

Carl walked inside as if he owned the place as usual. He glanced around noticing the apartment was completely empty and said, "I guess I caught you right before moved out."

I was angry! Carl was the last person that I expected to run into. I screamed, "What the hell do you want Carl? You tried ruining my life, because your life is so fucked up. I can't believe you have the audacity show your face here."

"Calm down Arnold, I didn't come here to start any problems."

This nigga must have lost his damn mind. What did he mean he didn't come to start any problems? I had to ask him that, "What do you mean you didn't come to start any problems? You already created a huge problem for me but thank God I was able to turn your lemons into lemonade."

Carl laughed with his arrogant ass and had the nerve to say, "Nigga, who do you think you are Beyonce? See you been hanging out with them faggots way too long, now they got you quoting Beyonce and shit. What are you the President of the Beehive now?"

I couldn't believe his arrogant ass. After everything he did to me he was standing in front of me making jokes and disrespecting me. This fool, really wanted me to catch a case, by knocking his ass out. Carl had me so heated. I was doing my best to practice restraint. I continued in a loud threatening voice, "Motherfucker, if you don't get your broke ass out this fucking apartment, and out my face, I am going to fuck you up, and I am not playing."

This nigga was still laughing and said, "Calm down playboy, I was just messing with you. No need for the violence. I heard about your new contract with that new team. I guess I was wrong about you gay people. Y'all sure know how to rally together and make the impossible happen. An all-gay basketball team affiliated with the NBA, that's a fucking miracle."

"Again, Carl what the fuck do you want, and what does any of this have to do with you?"

"Well you know I've always enjoyed our friendship. We were really close in college and I appreciate everything you did for me by allowing me to crash at your place and what not. I really just came here to apologize and see if we could work out our friendship."

"Man, I appreciate the apology, but it's a little too late for that. To be honest with you, when I look back at our relationship, I don't think you and me ever really had a real friendship. We were cool in college, but all you did was try to use me after I made it to the NBA. Then when you didn't get your way, you tried to destroy me. That isn't a true friendship Carl."

"Man, you have to understand that I haven't been in a good place ever since I had to stop playing ball because of my injury. You can't imagine the kinds of stuff that had been going through my head. My family and friends had been calling me washed up. I never made it to the NBA like you. I had to go play overseas. You already know the money playing overseas ain't no real money. I need you right now. Don't turn your back on me; I am really sorry Arnold."

I didn't have anything in my heart for Carl. The lust and sexual attraction had been completely diminished, ever since Carl showed his true colors. There was no going backwards for me, I was completely done with Carl. I politely escorting Carl out of the building and wished him luck on any future endeavors. I could slightly see a tear creeping out of the corners of his eyes, but I quickly turned my back toward him so I wouldn't feel so bad.

EPILOGUE

As much as Chaka wished she could find a way to get Pablo out of the mirror, and back inside his body, unfortunately that wasn't God's plan. She had to cast him out of the mirror and let his soul rest. Pablo's time on earth was finished. There was no reversing the black magic that put Pablo in place of Angel. The only thing that could be done was to get rid of all the black magic in the library, and in doing so Pablo would be gone forever. Chaka had finally realized what was missing from her anointing, and why she wasn't able to complete the removal ritual before today.

Her relationship with God had been at a standstill. Chaka needed to reconnect more with her heavenly Father and put aside any doubts of faith. Chaka had let life and its struggles come between her devotion. God was patient with Chaka, though. She was one of his chosen ones, and he wanted her *will* to be discovered on her own. As Chaka got better acquainted with Father Kind and the teachings she learned from her pastor at Alfred Street Baptist Church, she became the powerful crusader for Christ that was part of her destiny.

Chaka entered the men's bathroom for the final time. She knew what she had to do, and she was ready. When Chaka entered the restroom, the light came on and went back off within seconds. Pablo appeared through the mirror, he had that all-knowing look on his face. He knew what his former boss came in to do, and he was ready. Pablo didn't want to have to kill all those people, find a host and hijack their body. Pablo wasn't a killer, but he knew he had made a lot of mistakes in life, and he was ready to answer for them.

Chaka spoke first once she saw Pablo appear in the window, "I can't allow you to stay inside this mirror forever. As much as I prayed for another way to get you back into your body of flesh. That is something that I don't have the power to do. I wish I had better news for you, but I prayed for your soul and asked God to send you straight to heaven. I know my God is a merciful God, and there is no doubt in my mind once I break this curse you will be sent home to Glory. Life on earth is filled with pain, hardship, and struggle, have solace in knowing in Heaven you will not have to suffer any longer."

Pablo was in tears, because as much as he hoped he could reclaim his life, he knew the inevitable. He spoke up, "I am at peace with this; I really am. I've made my mistakes and I am ready to atone for them, in anyway God sees fit. There's no way I am going to listen to that witch whose magic is keeping me locked in this mirror and provide the lord of darkness innocent human sacrifices. I am not a killer and for what? My own selfish gain. It's not worth it and I won't do it, I just won't."

Chaka felt Pablo's pain and let him know he had one last visitor. "You have someone here who would like to speak with you before I do what needs to be done." Chaka opened up the door and in walked Arnold. Arnold had left abruptly after Pablo had been trapped inside the mirror. He thought he would never return back to the library again. However, Pablo had left a huge impression in Arnold's heart, and he wasn't able to walk away as easily as he thought he could.

Before Arnold could speak Pablo beat him to the punch, "I thought I would never lay eyes on you again. I don't want you to think that I was just trying to use and play you. That was never my intentions. I really did appreciate our friendship. I just thought you were too good to be true. I didn't think I deserved someone like you because of all the men that I have used and taken advantage of in my lifetime.

"You were so good to me, and I don't know what I did to deserve you. Everything the media said about me was true. I do have a history of male prostitution, stemming from a very young age. It's a lot harder for folk that live in the Dominican Republic. We don't have as many opportunities to make money like you do here in America. Escorting was never something I wanted to do, it was like a way of life for me."

Chaka left the restroom, so that Arnold and Pablo could be alone. She had one more fire to put out before she had to perform the hardest ritual of her life. Curtis was waiting for her in the lobby, when she got back upstairs. She greeted him, and they got down to business. "Thank you for coming in on your day off. I really appreciate you doing this for me."

Curtis replied, "It's no problem at all. I kind of feel somewhat responsible. I contacted Angel and he should be on his way to the library to meet me. He isn't doing very well these days without a permanent place to stay. He thinks I reached out to him to go sign a lease in my name, so he will have a place to live."

Chaka didn't condone lying, but she said, "Whatever you needed to say to get him down here, I guess is fine. Angel needs to pay for his actions, and since I can't get him back inside the mirror, the least I can do is make his life a living hell." Chaka motioned to two gentlemen who were also standing in the lobby of the library.

When the two men got in ear range Chaka continued, "This is Officer Calhoun and Roberts. They are from U.S. Immigration and Custom Enforcement. They are going to apprehend Pablo when he meets you out in front of the library." Although, Curtis and Chaka knew it was Angel in Pablo's body they had to play along. They both knew that the officers wouldn't be able to comprehend what had gone down at the library.

Curtis replied and said, "That's great! Pablo just texted me. He just got off the metro, and is walking toward the library now." Curtis walked out in front of the Library to meet Angel. He wasn't the least bit sorry that he was setting him up either. Curtis wanted to make up for his part in Jeffrey's death and his assistance in helping Angel escape from inside the mirror. When Curtis found out that Chaka had known all along about the paranormal activity going on in the library, he came clean about his involvement. He also said he had access to Angel and could reach him. That was when Chaka came up with the plan.

Curtis waited a few minutes and just as planned Angel came walking down the street. When Angel reached Curtis he said, "Now you know I can't be meeting you in front of where Pablo used to work. Folks are looking for me and this is very dangerous, but I was glad to hear that you decided to help me. Let's hurry up and get out of here, right away so nobody recognizes me. I have already picked the apartment building that I want to move into, and it's a quick trip on the Green Line Metro. There are some luxury apartments near the Georgia Avenue/Petworth Metro Station that I've been looking into."

Curtis was half listening and waiting for the abduction to occur so he could get away from Angel. Angel still freaked Curtis the hell out. When Curtis saw Chaka and the two gentlemen from immigration walk out the library, he started speaking. "Unfortunately, Angel I won't be helping you like we talked about."

Angel then looked into the direction of Curtis' eyes and saw Chaka walking toward him. Angel started getting upset, "What have you done Curtis? Did you set me up?"

Curtis didn't have the opportunity to respond. The officers quickly cornered Angel and one of them said, Mr. Hernandez please come with me. We've been looking for you for weeks for violating your green card status. You are being deported back to your home country of the Dominican Republic." He then handcuffed Angel and walked him to a black SUV that was parked in front of the Library.

You could hear angel crying and cursing, "What the hell have you done, Curtis? Why are you working with that bitch Chaka?" Neither Chaka nor Curtis responded to Angel's cries. They both just watched as Angel got forced into the backseat of the SUV, and it drove off.

Chaka then thanked Curtis for his assistance and Curtis left the library to enjoy the rest of his day off. Chaka on the other hand, went back to the bathroom to complete the final ritual so she could move on to bigger and better things.

When she'd gotten back downstairs Arnold was still there talking to Pablo through the mirror. Chaka interrupted their conversation and said, "It's time to say goodbye you two. I have to put an end to all this evil. This has gone on long enough, and I need to move on with my life.

"When Jesus and his disciples performed sacrifices in their day, they sacrificed animals not humans. Jesus' rituals were designed to feed the community during times when famine was high, and resources were limited. The rituals often times were performed at the temples where God's people congregated to hear the word of God. The sacrifice was for someone who had plenty to share and help feed the starving. When you give up something that belongs to you, and it's something of value, is the lesson Jesus was trying to teach to his followers on sacrifice.

"You see the devil tries to manipulate and reconstruct God's Holy practices. There is no such thing as a human sacrifice. Humans do not belong to people, so you have no right to sacrifice a life. Any human sacrifice is an abomination—it's murder—and what has transpired in the library all these years will end tonight, once and for all."